Golden Sovereign

By Dorothy Lyons

Illustrated by Wesley Dennis

Painting by Wayne Blickenstaff

SCHOLASTIC BOOK SERVICES

Published by Scholastic Book Services, a division
of Scholastic Magazines, Inc., New York, N. Y.

Copyright 1946 by Harcourt, Brace & World, Inc. This edition
is published by Scholastic Book Services, a division of Scholastic Magazines, Inc., by arrangement with Harcourt, Brace
& World, Inc.

5th printing................................March 1967
Printed in the U.S.A.

CONTENTS

CONTENTS

Golden Sovereign

CHAPTER ONE

THE CHESTNUT

PATCHES OF NEW GRASS were beginning to show through mud-tracked snow in the pasture. Two girls dressed in winter clothes, but with their jackets thrown open to the soft breeze, leaned on the fence while they watched the horses kick the winter's kinks out of their legs.

"They certainly look fit, Connie. Guess you've kept them in pretty good training all winter. Don't know that I've ever seen Silver Birch and Midnight Moon look better."

"They are all right. Sometimes I wonder if I keep them in trim, or they keep me in shape. What with all the book learning we've had to absorb senior year, I'd have been a stoop-shouldered bookworm but for them."

Di felt the strong spring sun on her throat as she tossed her head in laughter. It was difficult for her to picture her vitally alive friend care-worn and bookish. For a second her glance rested on Connie photographically and registered the

1

slender build that looked well in riding clothes, or a ski suit, or tennis shorts. Her friend's face was outstanding only for its expression of quiet purpose, but in the shining brown eyes sparkled an imp of Irish fun. Thick brown hair cut short looked so right Di involuntarily exclaimed,

"Don't ever let your hair grow long, Connie. It's just right this way."

She laughed anew at the look of amazement shot at her for getting so far off the beam, and jumped back to the topic.

"Don't worry, you won't come out of your cocoon a bookworm, Connie, so long as there's a horse on four—or maybe even three—legs in the world. You'd feel sure you could cure his fourth and make a winner of him."

Connie smiled ruefully, her thin face and quiet eyes lit by amusement at herself. "I'm not so sure. The way they've been passing out the homework this last semester, I've hardly had a chance to show Sliver what kind of a horse I want him to be."

"Sliver! Where is he? Don't you have him with the others any more?" Di's glance hastily swept the pasture before them.

"He's in the enclosure behind the barn," and Connie jerked her head to accent her statement. "Now that he's getting to be a big boy, he has a run to himself. Want to pay your respects, Di?"

Di's answer was to saunter toward the barn, and Connie leisurely followed. The two of them were as familar in and around Tyrone as the sun and the moon—or rather the moon and a star, for they always traveled together. Known to horsemen far beyond Tyrone, Michigan, and its environs, they were often referred to as The Black and The Chestnut, and each had won her spurs.

Di's early horsemanship had been learned many miles away in Virginia, before her parents were killed in a hunting accident and she had come to Tyrone to live. Since then she had mastered her fear of jumping and had helped Connie to win the black horse they had just left.

Connie, who had a way with a horse—any horse —had astonished horsemen near and far by capturing the love and devotion of a wild white mare and turning her into the slavelike Silver Birch. Then, to prove it had been no accident, Connie had changed the outlaw, Midnight Moon, from a wild, unmanageable mare to a tractable, spirited saddle horse.

Cutting through the barn, the girls came out by a smaller enclosure, bigger than a paddock but smaller than a pasture. Di's breath caught in her throat at the picture they saw.

Sliver, son of Silver Birch, stood like the illustration from a book on the ideal palomino. His shimmering golden coat fairly sparkled in the sunlight, every hair a tiny mirror of gold for the dazzling spring sun, and the breeze seemed to have sprung up for the sole purpose of tossing his luxuriant blond mane and tail about him in careless disarray. Perfect palomino markings of a white-striped nose and four carefully marked white stockings only accented his brilliance.

He posed proudly, as though carved from an old gold coin, but from the waggish gleam of his brown eyes Connie knew he was planning some prank.

"Whe-e-e-e," he shrilled to the world as he exploded into action. All four legs left the ground before he went tearing off like a meteor in full flight.

"Isn't he beautiful!" Di breathed almost prayerfully as she watched.

Sliver came around in a great circle and headed back toward Connie and Di. Never slackening his pace till the last moment, he misjudged the soft footing and slid along on his haunches in the mud. His look of amazement was so human the girls burst into whinnies of laughter themselves.

" 'Who pushed me?' eh, feller? Now your pants are all muddy." Connie laughed at him and would have petted him but he had to show them he didn't care.

Swapping ends as fast as he could, rearing high on his hind legs, and then rocking down to stand on his front and flourish his back legs in the air, Sliver's hoofs drummed out his spring song. Bucking, crowhopping, and shooting straight into the air, he added his spring dance to the program and the two earth-bound humans watched in fascination.

"How'd you like to be on him, Connie?" Di queried.

"I wouldn't," was the flat answer.

"Wouldn't like it?"

"No, wouldn't be on him—long!"

Satisfied that his audience was duly impressed, Sliver came mincing back, his nostrils fluttering like flower petals. Connie reached up and tousled his foretop.

"Feels pretty good to be out, doesn't it, young feller, me lad? No stall is big enough for such shenanigans, and spring's just the time for them!"

Connie's hands played over the golden head, stroked the petal-soft nose.

"You know, Di, book learning does have its points though."

"Connie, at a moment like this, why that?" her friend exclaimed.

"Well, when he was born I couldn't think of just the right name, so, being the son of Silver, we've called him Sliver. But the other day at school, I found the perfect name."

Impressed with the solemnity of the occasion, Di waited for Connie's pronouncement.

"Golden Sovereign." Deliberately Connie enunciated it, and then again. "I name thee Golden Sovereign," and a loving slap on his withers served as the sword stroke on his shoulder.

"That's super, Connie! He's golden enough, and in time he'll be a sovereign of some place, I know."

"Yes, he's practically eighteen-karat gold now,

and he'll be a king and reign long and happily, I'm sure." Connie's brown eyes burned intensely, and she almost seemed to be talking to herself. "Palomino stallions are valuable, and Golden Sovereign will be known far and wide, and his foals, and his foals' foals." She looked at Di.

"I suppose that sounds silly, doesn't it?"

"Ambitious maybe," Di countered, "but not silly. Aren't there a lot of good palomino stallions though?"

"Yes, but the difficulty with palominos is that it's a color that just happens in any breed of horse. There is an association that's working to standardize the palomino, but when you cross one with another color—or even with another of the same color—you can't be sure of always getting a palomino."

"So-o-o?"

"So that if Golden Sovereign consistently sires palominos, he'll soon be known all over. And if his sons do also, he'll help to establish the palomino as a real breed and not an accident of pigmentation."

"You've been reading books, Connemara McGuire!" Di accused her as those high-sounding words rolled off her tongue.

Connie's dusty-rose cheeks grew a shade redder. "Well, what if I have? I was just telling you why I'm sure that Golden Sovereign will be a king someday."

Di couldn't resist a sly nudge at her serious friend. Her eyes were wide and innocent. "How

can you tell that he'll sire such wonderful palominos? Maybe his sons and daughters will just
be like other palominos' foals. Did a leprechaun
tell you?"

"No, I just know, that's all," Connie intoned
dreamily. "Huh, what about a leprechaun?" The
dream faded from her eyes to be replaced by a
lively grin. "Oh, go along with you and stop teas-
ing. I'm dead serious though, but I will say 'if.'
If Golden Sovereign proves to be as good a sire
as I think he will, he'll be the real foundation
of my Shamrock Stables."

The Black and The Chestnut, inseparable in
school every other minute they could manage,
had discussed Connie's dream of raising horses
countless times. Today, however, seemed more
momentous than any other and Di pressed on.

"You haven't changed your plans about going
to college, have you? What would Pete say?"

"Oh, I'll be going to State College this fall. I'm
sorry I won't be at the university with you, but
what I really need is to learn all about crops
and animal husbandry and stuff, maybe even a
smattering of veterinary school too, so it's State
for me. It's lucky Pete is taking his engineering
degree there."

"The university has a good engineering school
too. Do you suppose Pete could have had anything else in mind when he decided on State instead?" Di wondered aloud.

Connie grew pink, but she ignored the thrust.
"Of course, I'm not through high school yet—I

have to limp through what's left of senior year. Guess I'll have to call a conference of Silver, Midnight, and Sliv—I mean Golden Sovereign—to see if they'll give me enough time off to do it."

"You do seem to have enough to keep you busy. But at that it isn't as bad as when you were following Silver across three counties, whistling love notes to her, or wearing yourself to a shadow working Midnight down to where she'd remember her manners."

"Glory! They were harrowing days!" Connie assented.

"Harrowing? Please don't get involved again—my nerves couldn't take it."

"Too bad about *your* nerves. But don't worry. I, Connemara McGuire, having reached the ripe old age of seventeen, the age of sense and discretion, will be a party no more to any such enterprises!" Connie's solemn manner promised better behavior than her merry eyes could guarantee.

"You'd better watch out, smarty. Don't forget that everything goes by threes."

"Not for me," Connie averred. "I'm a reformed character."

Further discussion was interrupted by a call from Connie's mother.

"Gir-rls. Time you were starting."

Reluctant to leave their spring pageant, they sauntered houseward, still deep in their horsey conversation.

Mrs. McGuire who had tarried on the back porch snapped them out of it.

"Land sakes, Connemara! One minute you're thrilled to death at the idea of going into the city with Di to buy your dress for the Valentine dance, and the next I practically have to snatch you off the back of a horse to get you started. Unless you've changed your mind and intend to whip up a stylish little number out of an old horse blanket, you'd better change your clothes and go."

No one was fooled by Mrs. McGuire's air of pretended exasperation at her only child, and Connie and Di hurried upstairs to get ready, their thoughts leaping ahead to the big school party Saturday night.

Connie's mother had scarcely had time to exchange two recipes with a visitor before the girls were back downstairs, ready to leave.

"You have the money your father gave you?"

Connie nodded and patted her purse.

"What color do you think you'll get?"

"Oh-h, green maybe, or gold. Pete says I look nice in either."

"Well, good luck then—and don't lose your purse." Mrs. McGuire looked fondly after her daughter, who seemed so grown-up one minute and such a child the next.

Mrs. Tabor watched the girls depart with less approval.

"Connemara is going to buy her party dress without your assistance? Do you think that is wise?"

"No, I suppose not," Mrs. McGuire sighed, "but it did seem the only way out today. It's a holiday for her and her last chance to shop before the party, but I just have to be at home today because Jim had to go away and the man might come about the insurance."

"Aren't you afraid Connemara will buy something unsuitable?" The words seemed to slide disdainfully off Mrs. Tabor's nose rather than issue from her mouth.

"My goodness, yes! But not afraid the way you are. I'm afraid she'll come home with new riding boots or breeches, instead of the wrong dress." Mrs. McGuire's hearty chuckle made her caller's fears slightly ridiculous, and the conversation passed to safer topics.

Meanwhile Connie and Di were rolling along on top of the world. Di had her Aunt Lou's convertible for the day and the miles slipped past easily. Nearing the city Di turned off the main highway.

"Where're you going, Di? That's the way in— you ought to know by now."

"This's a cutoff Uncle Dan showed me the other day. Takes you right into the business section without so much traffic. Of course the part of town it goes through isn't very classy, but it's direct."

Grumbling softly to herself about getting lost, Connie leaned back and watched the city go by. With each block its looks got worse as suburban cottage changed to tenement and tenement changed to warehouse and produce firms.

" 'S funny," Di muttered. "We should have hit

that through street by now. Maybe it's off this
way," she decided hopefully as she swung the car
around a corner.

It wasn't, but not far ahead the street was lined
solid with parked cars. Curiosity lightened Di's
foot on the gas, and drawing abreast of the commotion, her foot slipped off altogether. A not-too-
tidy stable stood back from the street. The space
before it was crowded with people and over it
hung a limp, weathered sign which proclaimed:
MAMMOTH AUCTION STABLES. AUCTION
EVERY THURSDAY. BRING YOUR HORSES AND
MULES HERE FOR HIGHEST PRICES!

The Black and The Chestnut eyed each other
silently for an instant before the car slid in and
stopped at the curb. Picking their way through
the crowd they found a spot that afforded a good
view of the sales ring, but at the same time allowed them to watch the crowd—always one of
the best parts of an auction. The Mammoth Auction Stables evidently catered to teamsters, truck-
ers, and delivery firms, for the horses all were
draft-horse type. Connie and Di looked on for a
while, but soon the novelty began to wear off.

"Let's get going," Di whispered. "Unless you've
taken a fancy to some natty little mule and want
to put in a bid."

"All right, I'm not really in the market for a
draft horse." Connie turned to go, but the auctioneer's flow of superlatives checked her.

"Now, gentlemen—and ladies," with a bow toward the girls. "We are offering an unusually fine

horse. A little on the light side perhaps for heavy work, but we feel exceptionally fortunate to be able to present this little mare for your consideration.

"She's a trifle run-down, but if any of you is looking for a light harness horse, say for a delivery wagon, here's your opportunity. She's not old—look at her teeth yourself; she's gentle and well-mannered under harness—won't kick your wagon to pieces or run away. She's—"

"O.K., O.K., trot her out and let's get started," a voice called out.

"You're that anxious to see her, eh? All right, Bill, bring Number 47 out."

After the auctioneer's build-up, Connie expected to see something like a Morgan. At her first sight of the scrawny, ill-kempt bag of bones that was led into the ring a soft "Oh-h-h" of pity escaped from Connie's lips. Probably standing not over 15.1 hands in new shoes (if she ever had them) the mare was so thin her skin visibly slid over every rib as she breathed.

"Run-down, he says," Di muttered. "Look at the sores on her mouth, and the galls where the skin has worn through between collar and bones."

"That boy'd better hold onto her tight or a strong breeze will blow her over," Connie growled.

"Come, come, gentlemen—and ladies," the auctioneer bawled. "Let's have a bid on this dandy mare. What do I hear?"

"Ha!" from someone was all he heard.

"Bill, lead her around a little so they can see her better."

The mare hobbled after Bill as he circled the ring. Because of sore feet she stepped as if on eggs, and as Bill turned too short she winced sharply. For an instant as they swung around her eyes looked directly at Connie. Battered though her body was, her gallant spirit glowed strong and plain, and the girl stretched out her arm and ran her hand softly along the mare's chestnut flanks.

Back from where they started, Bill and the mare stopped of one accord. From somewhere far back in the past her memory prompted her to advance her front feet a pace, her neck reached forward and up, ears pricked forward, and even the dirty, fuzzy brush that was called a tail arched ever so slightly. Perhaps no one but Connie recognized those feeble efforts as the mare's attempt to stretch like a show horse, but Connie's eyes misted.

"She's seen better days," she whispered to her friend.

"Oh, Con, don't be sentimental. Of course, she wasn't born just like that, but she couldn't have come this low without having been pretty far down the scale to begin with. Come on, it's getting late."

"Di, didn't you notice—" Connie began, but halted.

"Five dollars."

The crowd turned to locate what optimist had

spoken. A hard-looking man with a three days'
growth of beard which looked as greasy as his
clothes had come forward. With eyes set so close
together he almost seemed cross-eyed, he scanned
the mare.

"If that's the way he takes care of himself, the
poor horse won't ever get a brushing—or any bed-
ding. I wonder who he is?" Connie mused.

"That's Jenks for Junk. He must have a tidy
income from the hides of horses he kills from over-
work," the man beside her told his companion as
though in answer to her thought. "That nag won't
last him a month, but he can't resist a bargain."

"Ten dollars!" Connie almost looked to see who
else was bidding before she realized she had
spoken.

Jenks for Junk stared nearsightedly at her and
reflected, as the auctioneer badgered him.

"Ten dollars I have, do I hear fifteen—fifteen?
Who'll give me fifteen?"

"Fifteen," Jenks conceded.

"Fifteen dollars for this dandy little mare. Fifteen. Who'll say twenty? Twenty dollars—why,
she's a steal at that price. Do I hear twenty?"

"Twenty," Connie nodded, doing some rapid
calculations.

"Twenty, the little lady says. Let me have
twenty-five. Who'll make it twenty-five? Twenty
once, twenty twice—" His hammer poised in the
air.

"Twenty-two," Jenks squeezed.

"Now he's just being cussed," Connie's neighbor remarked.

"Twenty-two, do I hear twenty-five? What about it, miss? Will you make it twenty-five?"

Di shook her head violently at Connie and scowled darkly, but her friend paid no attention.

"Twenty-four." The resolution in Connie's voice surprised herself as much as the bystanders.

"Twenty-four I've got. Will you give me twenty-six? Do I hear twenty-six?" The auctioneer looked hopefully at Connie's opponent.

"Twenty-five," he growled.

"Twenty-five fifty," Connie snapped without waiting for the auctioneer's prompting. "That is, twenty-five dollars and fifty cents!"

Jenks for Junk dusted his hands eloquently. "She's not worth that to me. Besides, I don't need another horse."

"Nor do I—this one anyway," Connie thought with consternation while the sales hammer banged to emphasize her rashness.

"Now you've done it, Connie. But why the fifty cents on top of twenty-five dollars?" Di inquired.

"Because that's part of my allowance next month sometime. Well, I guess she's all mine," Connie said with forced cheerfulness.

"Let's hurry up and do whatever we have to, or we'll never get to the stores in time to find what you want this aft," Di urged, but at the look on her friend's face she realized her mistake.

"There's no hurry now. We won't have to go

any farther today." Connie stepped forward to claim the latest addition to Shamrock Stables.

"The Chestnut sure bought herself a chestnut this time," Di murmured.

CHAPTER TWO

McGUIRE MADNESS

BACK SO SOON?" Mrs. McGuire called out when she heard Connie and Di come in the house. "Hurry and show me what you bought. You must have had good luck to find one so fast."

She looked expectantly at Connie, who stood in the doorway.

"Mom, which horse blanket d'ya think would look best on me?"

"Which horse blanket! What do you—? Connemara McGuire, what did you do? Lose that money?"

In answer, Connie motioned toward the window and, turning, Mrs. McGuire saw a car and trailer turning into the driveway.

"My land! Another horse—at least I guess it's meant to be a horse. Where on earth did you ever find such a nag?"

"She's not a nag—at least she didn't used to be. Once upon a time she was a fine horse—that is, I feel sure she was, but I can't really prove it. Come on down to the barn if you want the story. This man very generously offered to drop her off here—she'd never have made it herself in a thousand years—and I don't want to delay him."

"Connemara, Connemara! Any horse is or has been a good horse to you. Why couldn't you have taken an interest in goldfish, or birds, or even cats, if you're always going to be bringing them home? But horses!" her mother chided. "You realize there'll be no more money for a dress? That you'll have to wear one of your old ones to the dance?"

"Sure, Mom, I know. But I wouldn't have enjoyed myself wearing the best dress in the world if I'd let that horrible old creature buy the mare."

Once unloaded, the newcomer was made as comfortable as possible in a box stall and her handmaidens leaned over the door to watch her.

"She certainly is the sorriest specimen of horseflesh I think I've ever seen," Mrs. McGuire flatly stated, "and I can think of no exceptions. But she does look familar to me. Now I've got it: it's the Four Horsemen of the Apocalypse who ride horses like her."

"I'll bet she thinks she's died and gone to heaven already," Di commented.

A loose box six inches deep with clean straw, a mangerful of fragrant hay, and even some grain, with kind, quiet voices round her, must have seemed a veritable heaven beyond heaven to the battered crowbait. With a greediness born of hunger and irregular feeding times, she lost no time in gobbling up the grain. Long before she had finished the hay, weariness overcame hunger, and the scarred, bony body was lowered into the straw with a grunt and a sigh.

"Named her yet, Connemara?" her mother asked. "Though what you'd want to name her for I can't see. All she looks fit for is a bullet through the head to put her out of her misery!"

"Goodness, Mom, even a condemned criminal always gets a good dinner first. But I'm not so sure we ought to kill her. I'll bet she used to be a good horse."

Hoots of derision from Di and her mother were her only answer.

"You could call her Sleeping Beauty," Di suggested, looking down at the bag of bones in the straw.

"Or My Valentine for the dress you won't wear to the party," her mother contributed.

"How about Lost Lady?" Connie asked hopefully. "She's sort of lost, and you can tell she used to be a lady."

"*You* can tell, you mean. Anybody else'd get eyestrain trying to see it." Di prodded her friend again. "Guess we might as well get used to the idea. Connie's got a fixation again, and just this morning I warned her not to. Nobody ever takes my advice," she concluded dolefully.

"Well, Miss Fifth Horseman, if you're going to have anything to wear to that party Saturday, we'd better get back to the house and go through your clothes to see what we can patch up for you."

Mrs. McGuire shooed them away from the stall and, joking though her tone had been, her eyes were as tender as Connie's when they left. Di went back in the barn for a minute.

"Just thought I'd put a little hay on the floor so she could nibble a bit while she's lying down if she wants," she murmured into space when she caught up with the others.

The next morning early Connie was down at the barn giving Shamrock Stables a second look when her father came in.

"You didn't pick out a very stylish occupant for our only empty stall," he observed mildly.

"I know it, Dad. She does look pretty awful, but you wouldn't have stood by and let that filthy old brute buy her either, and you know it, Dad McGuire."

"No, I guess I wouldn't. What do you think you'll do with her though? Mother says you wouldn't hear of having her put to sleep."

"Can't we keep her awhile, Dad? She might shape up into something we could sell to a good home and make a little money on her. We could use it, couldn't we?"

"We certainly could! Got a lot of horses here

eating their heads off, and except for the fun you get out of 'em, they don't bring in any income."

"I know, but just wait until Shamrock Stables gets going, and then we'll get some of it back. And pretty soon the pasture'll be good enough to turn this one out and 'twon't hardly cost us anything," Connie pleaded convincingly.

"Still figuring on raising horses for sure? We'll have to be making some plans one of these days if you are. Here we've already got this barn filled and you've hardly started. Time enough though, I guess, before we'll need it. You're sure you won't change your mind and decide to go into the city to work when you're through school?" he quizzed.

"Sure I'm sure. You ought to know me by now, Dad. Once I take a notion, I hang onto it like a puppy to a stick."

"Yes, I ought to know you by now, Connemara," he agreed dryly. "I only hope you don't decide someday to ride around the world. But if you do," he added, "I'll feel it's all right to address a post card to you and your horse in Arabia.

"Let's have a look at your new horse then, if you're set on keeping her."

Sleeping-Beauty My-Valentine Lost-Lady was led into the paddock and tied to a post so that Connie and her father could give her the once-over. Some food and a good rest seemed to have perked her up a little, for instead of standing in a daze, she looked about with interest and watched them as they moved about her. Connie brought brush and currycomb and went to work industriously on the rough, moth-eaten coat.

"Look, Dad, she likes me already," Connie cried with delight as she felt the tired old head rest on her back.

"She's just taking it easy," he scoffed, but his words made no impression on Connie's ballooning interest.

"Got nice markings," he remarked. "Legs don't seem too bad, but the front ones are pretty puffy. May go down though with care. Let's pull off these old shoes and trim up her hoofs," he told himself and forthwith brought the tools.

"I wish it were warmer, so I could give her a bath," Connie complained. "She'd feel lots better, and so would I, but I don't dare do it now. Better put some medicine on those sores.

"What'll I name her, Dad? We can't just call her 'her' all the time." Connie recounted the sarcastic suggestions made the previous evening.

"I don't know what to call her, but I'll bet she calls you Lady Luck all right. And at a time when she probably thought her luck had run out," her father mused.

"Lady Luck. I like that, and I still think that I was as lucky as she was. I think I'll name her Lady Luck."

In her enthusiasm, Connie spoke the name with great distinctness. To her surprise, the mare turned her head to look at her.

"Dad, she knows her name! I'll bet she's been

called Lady before. Have you, old lady, or were you a young lady then? I wish you could tell me about it, where you were born and who you belonged to and how you happened to leave your nice home," Connie crooned to the old mare. "Lady Luck you are and Lady Luck you'll be. I feel it in my bones."

Her father had finished his work and stepped back. "Might as well put her back in now. All she needs for some time is food and rest, but the first really warm day we'd better worm her and put her off by herself. That fuzzy tail is apt to mean worms."

"First I think I'll clip her mane and tail. They don't add a bit to her appearance, and they might as well grow out new," Connie planned. Soon she was snipping busily on tail and mane and fetlocks, in fact any place she could spot an extra tuft to invite her scissors.

The following evening Connie dressed in her latest creation, a product of her mother's ingenuity. To her last year's party dress had been added a contrasting jacket from another, and she spent anxious moments in front of her mirror trying to achieve a different hairdo.

"I do look all right, don't I, Mom?" she pleaded for reassurance. "Of course they'll all know it isn't a new dress, but I think the combination is striking. And after all, my hair is different!"

"You look fine, Connemara, and Pete is so used to seeing you in riding clothes, anything else will be a novelty," Mrs. McGuire assured her daugh-

ter, whose sparkling eyes and rosy look of excitement would have transformed any dress into
a party dress.

"Do you think—oh, there he comes now," Connie exclaimed as a car drove in. "Should I leave
my hair this way or do it over like I generally
wear it?" she asked in a flurry.

"Unless you want Peter to play a few games of
checkers with your father while he's waiting,
you'd better leave it that way," Mrs. McGuire
good-naturedly advised. "It looks nice—a different style, too."

"Hi, Con," Pete greeted her gaily, shoving a
tissue-wrapped package at her. "Be my valentine.
Hey, I thought you told me on the phone that
your new dress was brown, sort of. You're not
in brown—or aren't you the girl I came to get?"

"I didn't say my dress was brown at all, Pete
Kendall. I only said that my purchase was
brown. And it is! Come on and I'll show you."
Connie started for the back door.

"Connemara, for heaven's sakes—" her mother
began, only to give up at the sound of the back
door closing.

Going through the yard in the dark, Pete took
Connie's arm to help her. Barely able to repress
a giggle, as she thought of the thousands of
times she had negotiated that same path in all
weathers without mishap, she demurely allowed
herself to be guided to the barn door.

Once inside, Pete snapped on the light and,

pointing at Lady Luck, Connie announced, "There stands my new dress in all her glory."

"Glory!" Pete whistled through his teeth. "Where'd you dig that up from? And I mean 'dig up.'"

"*Et tu*, Pete," Connie exclaimed in sorrow. "Now I thought you'd be one who could tell a good horse when you saw one." She recounted briefly how Lady Luck had come into her life.

"I don't blame you for forgetting about your dress, Connie. Poor old girl looks as though she's had some rough times, but as for being a princess in disguise, I don't know." Pete shook his head doubtfully.

"You come out tomorrow, and I'll show you what convinced me," Connie promised.

"Come on, we'd better get going. Di and Denny probably have their fingernails chewed off to the elbow by now," she remembered.

Di gave Connie a reassuring nod of approval when they met.

"Enter the Fifth Horseman," Pete proclaimed grandly as they walked in the door, and news of the latest "McGuire madness" soon made the rounds. All her friends had to have a blow-by-blow account of her latest adventure and the new mare, so Connie had no time to regret not having a new dress to flaunt.

CHAPTER THREE

LADY LUCK

AFTER CHURCH THE NEXT DAY, Connie turned her attention to Lady Luck again, who by then was relaxing into her new-found comfort. She was less likely to jump at sudden noises, and though she still spent much of her time lying down, she showed an interest in barn activities.

"It's good that you do take it easy, Lady Luck. It'll get some of the strain and puff out of your legs and the soreness out of your hoofs faster," Connie confided to her patient. "There're a lot of doubting Thomases we've got to show a thing or three before we're through."

Time and again brush and currycomb had gone over Lady's rough hair, and each time they filled with dust and fuzz and flakes of dried skin.

"Tomorrow I'll buy you a little cottonseed meal. That'll put the old gloss back into your coat. Or, of course, I could take you to town for a hot-oil treatment!"

It was impossible for Connie to work around

any horse without talking the whole business over with the object of her attentions, and Lady Luck came in for her share of conversation. Her large brown eyes, made larger by the bones and hollows around them, watched the slight girl who had so miraculously come into her life; and the better acquainted they were, the more she liked her.

The tone of her voice was pleasant and reassuring. Her touch was gentle as it went from nose to tail, first one side, then the other. Even the smell of her, so different from that repulsive creature who used to harness her, reminded Lady of something dim and almost forgotten: tweeds and grain blended with the pleasant odor of other well-kept horses, straw and hay mixed into a fragrance of their own. Lady's eyes closed as her memory strove to pierce the curtain that had dropped between then and now. A voice brought her back to reality.

"Hello. Anybody here?"

"Ain't nobody here but just us horses." Connie used the time-honored joke to answer Pete's hail.

They smiled comfortably at each other. Connie and Pete, who had been friends for years and who had seen each other at the worst as well as the best, were concerned only with the business of the day.

"Where's that diamond in the rough, or should I say your princess in disguise?" Pete bantered. "Let's see what the harsh light of day does to this lady's looks."

Connie slipped a rope around Lady Luck's neck, reluctant to put a halter on the bony head, and led the mare into the yard while Pete looked searchingly at her.

"Hm-m, she might be built into a good horse," he admitted.

"There, that's what I say!" Connie exclaimed, but she had not heard all.

"Yes, you might build her into a horse—anyway you've got a good framework started."

"Anything for a gag, eh?" she complained. "But seriously, what d'ya think?"

"What's that secret proof you promised to show me today? Gotta have all the available information to make a decision, you know."

"I'm not sure whether she'll do it with a neck rope instead of a halter, but I'll try."

Looping the loose end around Lady's nose to simulate a halter, Connie pulled gently and vibrated it. Was it already her improved condition, or did Lady strike the pose more definitely than she had at the auction? Forefeet advanced slightly, her ears stiffened to attention, and even her neck changed from its thin, straight line to a barely perceptible arch. Connie's eyes looked the question, but rather than lay herself open to another joke she waited for Pete to speak.

"Yes, sir. Yes, sir! Con, we've really got something here."

Putting that "we" away for future consideration, Connie cried, "Oh, I'm so glad you think so, Pete. I couldn't bear to have her put away, but there've been so many cracks about the poor old thing, I began to wonder if maybe I might be a little touched on the subject of horses."

"Of course, I'm not denying that, Connie," he said—and ducked, "but no horse would stretch like that unless she had been trained to or had it in her breeding. Certainly I wouldn't have her killed."

"She's not terribly old," Connie added eagerly. "I can't tell as accurately as Dr. Casey can, but look. Her teeth look like about nine or ten years old," Connie judiciously stated.

"Is that right? Sure enough." Pete peered into Lady's mouth. "Blazes, she'll make a good brood mare for the stables. Why, that's just a horse's prime of life," he cried with mounting excitement.

"If we prime her with enough hay and grain," Connie snatched her chance for a joke. "Guess that's about all we can do—and clear up her galls—for quite a while."

"Ye-e-s, but just our knowing won't do any good. We'll have to prove that she comes of good stock to increase her value. Wonder if we could back-track and find out where she came from?"

"We could try, Pete. That auction stable must know who they got her from, and that person where he got her—"

"And on and on and on until we get back to the beginning," he finished.

"But let's keep it quiet, Pete, or we'll have to take a lot of ribbing. There'll be plenty anyway," Connie acknowledged. "Everyone'll have to eat crow though if we can come up with proof that Lady Luck's luck hasn't all been bad."

"You bet! McGuire and Kendall, Detectives Extraordinary. Horses a Specialty," Pete proclaimed. "Sure and begorra, Lady Luck it will be for Shamrock Stables. I'll stop by that auction place on my way home just in case there's someone there. I'll phone you tonight," he promised as they returned Lady to her stall.

"Where are the other horses? They'll be offended if we don't pay our respects to them too, and Lady Luck seems to need a little shut-eye now."

"Out here," Connie directed, opening the back door toward the paddock.

Silver Birch and Midnight Moon walked toward them, obviously looking for a handout; nor were they disappointed. Pete, however, crossed toward the other paddock.

"Jiminy, Sliver's a beauty. Your Irish luck was running high when he was born, but then it always seems to. Look at him! Perfect palomino markings, as glorious a color as the sun-god himself, such hair in his mane and tail as a chorus girl would envy—"

"And the disposition of an angel," Connie finished. "I am lucky. Sometimes it scares me. Everybody's due for a certain amount of bad luck. Suppose it's all being stored up and someday when I'm not looking, boom! everything hits me at once."

"Not you, me darlint," Pete denied, sounding more like a vaudeville Irishman than a son of the old sod. "Anyone born Connemara McGuire has all the little people on her side and she can't lose.

"If Sliver has the disposition of an angel, he shouldn't be hard to break. When are you going to start?"

"You ought to know me better than that! I started a year and a half ago. When he was a day old," Connie continued at Pete's look of surprise. "From the day he was born I've been working with him and already he's used to a halter, he leads like a lamb, even a bridle isn't too strange to him. I know what you mean though, and as soon as school is out—probably before that, as soon as the weather gets nice—he'll graduate from kindergarten into first grade."

"I hope you're one hundred per cent right about his disposition, Connie, for breaking a stallion could be pretty rough business for a pint-size number like you. Any time I can help, all you have to do is yell. Fact is, when school's out I'll not be far off anyway, as long as Asthma can sputter along."

"You ought to know then that his name isn't Sliver any more. From now on he is officially Golden Sovereign, but his old friends can call him Sliver if they want to."

Pete whistled admiringly. "Sa-a-y, that's all right! Gives him something to live up to, doesn't it?"

While they talked, the girl and redheaded boy had been moving around the object of their admiration until his patience was exhausted. With head high and his tail flying like a banner, Golden Sovereign galloped across the pasture.

"How about a short ride, Pete," Connie suggested. "Silver and Midnight need a little work, and it's been so soupy under foot lately they haven't been out in quite a while."

"You don't think I'll be thrown, do you?" Pete queried with mock anxiety. "I'm just a boy from the city, you know."

"Not you. Dr. Casey'd disown you if anything on four feet that whinnies ever outbluffed you."

They worked while they talked, and the two horses were soon ready, Connie's saddle by tacit agreement on Silver and the spare one on Midnight. The horses were equally eager for an outing and pranced about, once Connie and Pete had mounted.

"The footing would be better on the road, but let's ride in the woods. I like to see them beginning to come to life, and maybe one or two flowers will be out," the girl suggested, and the horses' heads were accordingly turned into the lane.

Instead of thudding hoofs, the riders grew accustomed to the squish-squish of sloppy footing, but around them spring held out her promise on every hand. Snowbanks were dissolving miraculously, every gulley had its own rivulet chattering to it, ice on the lake had a tired gray complexion, but best of all was the dome of blue from which the sun poured down on the winter-sick earth.

"Has anyone else ever ridden Silver Birch, Connie?" Pete inquired after watching the complete understanding that flowed between girl and horse.

"I don't think so, unless it was the old fellow who raised her, which I doubt; or someone at Mr. Drummond's while he had her. No matter how many horses I ever have, Silver is the one I'll pick for a perfect ride. I've never tried it, but it seems as if I could guide her just by thinking which way I want to go without even touching the reins."

"Life's funny," Pete mused. "Do you suppose if you'd never joined the Pegasus Patrol and wanted a riding horse of your own, you'd have discovered what a way you have with horses? Lots of people go for years without ever knowing just what they're good for, but you, before you were even in high school, found out and knew what you wanted to do when you grow up."

Connie thought she detected a touch of wistfulness in Pete's voice, perhaps only because she knew his problems. The son of rich parents who had looked on him much as a business investment that must be watched and regulated in order to mature at the proper date at full value, he had had to look to friends for understanding and companionship. Any deviation from his parents' ways was frowned down, and apparently there had been discussion of his future recently.

"It comes to everyone sooner or later, Pete, and if I hadn't discovered for myself through Silver Birch, I might have waited for years before I knew what I wanted to do. It just takes time, but there's no good worrying over it."

"Well, if Silver hadn't showed you, you'd have had a second chance when you made that bet with

Puckett that you could retrain Midnight out of her wild ways well enough to win a first or second ribbon in a horse show or forfeit Silver—" he began.

"If I hadn't had Silver Birch, don't think Jed Puckett would have bet his horse against mine, not while I was riding clumsy old Ted like I used to. See, it's mostly chance, and when it happens—it happens, is all," Connie concluded lamely and then diverted the conversation to happier channels.

"How's your Waltz Dream these days?" she asked, referring to Pete's own horse, his parents' only concession to a taste that differed from theirs.

"She's in topnotch condition. But you know what? When I came last night I was going to ask if you would board her for me, and look what I found in the only empty stall. That caricature of a horse!"

"Why ever do you want to bring her out here? You couldn't ride her half so often."

"But it'd be more fun when I did. That city stable bunch is stuffy, and the country would be good for Dreamy," he finished airily. "Guess it's no go as long as the lost princess got there first."

"No, I guess not," Connie agreed, but had Pete observed closely there was a gleam in Connemara's eyes that usually presaged some new step.

The westering sun had lost much of its warmth, and unconsciously the horses had been headed toward the barn where they were stabled and cared for, and Pete reluctantly went back to his city home.

With one eye on the clock, Connie mentally

followed him back, figuring when he'd stop at the auction stables and how soon he might phone about Lady's last owner. At last, after she thought Pete had had time to make the round trip three times, the phone rang.

"Connie, this is me. Sorry to take so long. The stables were shut up tight, but I got the man's home address and tracked him down. He said that Lady Luck had come in a bunch of stock from that sales yard the other side of town. I went there, but it was closed. I'll be home from State next weekend and I'll stop there before I come out Saturday—you're going to be home, aren't you?"

"Sure, Pete. I'll be here, a shadow of my former self if they keep pouring on the homework. I'll keep my fingers crossed that you'll have better luck next time."

CHAPTER FOUR

McGUIRE & COMPANY

A FEW DAYS LATER Connie found an opening for broaching her newest scheme to her father They were working together in the barn, and when he paused to light his pipe she spoke.

"Dad, Pete wanted us to board Waltz Dream for him—that is, he did before he knew about Lady Luck."

"Not a chance of it now, as long as you intend to keep that ex-horse."

"You know, Dad, I've been thinking. We live pretty close to the big summer colony at the lake, and we're not too far from the city. I'll bet we could make quite a lot of extra money by taking boarders. Either people going away who want to put their horses out in the country, or some like Pete who would rather drive a little farther instead of riding in the city."

"And where do you propose we put these horses —in tents?" he asked dryly.

"No, but if we built another barn now, we could be paying for it with the money from the boarders, and it'd be all ready when we really get going on Shamrock Stables," she finished with a rush.

"What do you suggest using for money? Just at the moment I don't have enough in my jeans to build a new barn. Have you?"

"I've thought of that, Dad. You've got my college money for next year all put away, haven't you?"

Mr. McGuire nodded shortly.

"We could use that then for a start, and if it wasn't enough the boarders could help us pay for it."

"With a lot of extra horses eating their heads off, where'd we get the hay? I don't want to plant any more of the farm to hay, and now that we have Lady Luck it'll be nip and tuck as to whether we'll have enough for our own stock at the end of a long winter." Mr. McGuire felt sure Connie would have some answer for this and waited to see what it would be.

A deep breath and a gulp launched her deeper into her plans. "The old Clinton place next door has been idle for a long time. Could we—do you think—why not buy or lease that or farm it on shares?"

For an uneasy minute Connie thought all her plans would be swept away in laughter, but her father's reply was serious enough.

"Getting pretty ambitious, aren't you, Connemara? All of this takes money, and while I grant that your plans sound sensible, suppose something went wrong and we couldn't pay for all this. What'd we do then?"

"But nothing will go wrong, Dad. I just know it won't. And next year we ought to have some money coming in. You see, if we mate Golden Sovereign with the mares we'll have some dandy colts for sale, and palominos bring high prices."

"Of course, you're sure they'll all be palominos. You feel it in your bones," he said in concert with his eager daughter.

"I do. Honest I do, Dad. I can't explain how I know. Maybe it's like Pete said. All the little people are helping me."

"Well, I'll think it over, Connemara, but I don't see how we could swing both the barn and the extra land, and one wouldn't be any good without the other. I'd hate to use your college money anyway, but I'll see. After all, the farm will be yours someday, and I'd like to have it in shape the way you want it. I'll see," he repeated, picked up a pitchfork, and left.

After supper the McGuires met in a family conclave on the proposed expansion. For Mrs. McGuire's benefit, her husband outlined Connie's scheme, with frequent additions from her, and concluded with, "I'm not in favor of it, but Connemara has been a partner of McGuire and Company since she raised the money for your operation, and each of you has a vote. What do you think, Mother?"

Mrs. McGuire was silent for several minutes. Connie's fingers were crossed tightly for luck while she waited for her mother's verdict.

"Connemara, you do understand that both of us are thinking of your own good, don't you? I wouldn't want to see you wait a year before going to college when all your friends are starting this fall, but agreeing to that, we could only swing it if Jim could farm the Clinton place on shares, and I'm afraid that's impossible. Others have asked to do it before, but never got permission. Jim, you could try tomorrow, but it'd be out of the question to buy or lease it on top of the expense of building a barn."

There it was left, pending Mr. McGuire's report, and Connie couldn't get home from school fast enough the next night. From the curt, negative shake of his head, Connie guessed that, in spite of his argument against it, he had really wanted to do it himself. Instead of her doing homework that evening, Connie wrestled with money-making schemes, but short of selling her horses no idea presented itself. She even considered entering every contest advertised, but remembering a friend's unhappy experience several years ago, she discarded the idea.

Small wonder that when Pete's bright thatch and merry gray eyes appeared Saturday, he greeted her with, "Hello there, Miss Cloud-across-the-Sun. What's the eclipse about today?"

They perched on a fence while Connie outlined her lovely plans that had come to naught. Pete chewed a stalk of hay thoughtfully before he spoke.

"You'd really rather build a barn than come to college next year? Remember I'm there unprotected from all the campus sirens, and I've been counting on your being there next year to beat 'em off."

This was an angle Connie had overlooked in her zeal to get Shamrock Stables off to a good start. A pause was necessary before she answered.

"I guess I'd like to do both, Pete. But if I'm really going on with Shamrock Stables—and I can't think of any other way I'd rather earn a living— now's the time to do it right. Why, we haven't room for another horse. If Di rode out to stay all night, we'd have to bed Dixie down in the passageway. That's a fine situation for a growing stable to be in.

"And it's too bad about your needing protection. I'll bet you do all right for yourself with those sirens. You probably sound like a four-alarm fire yourself, Pete Kendall. Anyway, it looks like I'll be there next fall since we can't work the next farm, and a barn's no good without hay in it!"

She mused dreamily, "It's a sweet little place, too. Springy marshes for continuous pasture, good rich fields for hay and grain, woods—oh well, no use thinking about it."

Pete listened quizzically, but as she continued her praises of the unattainable acres, his look was tinged with regret. Suddenly it cleared.

"Say, have you forgotten about my report on Lady Luck's past?"

"Yes, Pete, no. I mean yes. Anyway what is it?" Connie exclaimed, nearly falling off her perch in eagerness.

"Not good. I stopped there today on my way out of town, but that fellow said he had gotten the mare—Maude he called her—from some laundry in the city. He couldn't recall the name, but said it was something like a breakfast food. I couldn't find any names like that in the phone book, so where do we go from here?"

"Blessed if I know. But my brain is overworked today, and not in very good condition. Let's give Golden Sovereign a little workout and then think."

Sunny weather for a week had changed the field from a bog to the point where it could be used. Connie and Pete began, perhaps for their own satisfaction, by giving Golden Sovereign a thorough grooming until he glistened like new-threshed wheat straw. His halter was then slipped on, and he stepped into the ring for his first real lesson.

"I'm sure he's used to a rope by now, but the longer longe rope may be different, so we'd better let him get acquainted with it first," the earnest girl suggested.

The trio accordingly halted in the open field, and Connie slipped the coil down from her shoulder. Golden Sovereign snorted and edged off a few steps, but Connie encouraged him with meaningless chatter. As soon as his wariness had vanished, she substituted the snap from the longer rope for his own lead rope, being careful to keep it tightly bundled together so that no loose ends would frighten him.

The colt nearly looked cross-eyed down his nose trying to see this new object, but otherwise he accepted it calmly.

"Pete, if you'll be anchor man in case he goes into the highland fling, I'll start him around the circle. Don't pay the rope out too far. We'd better keep him in a pretty small circle first."

Golden Sovereign stood at right angles to the lead rope, still eying it warily lest it spring at him, but his fears dwindled to zero as Connie patted and talked to him. Her right hand grasped the rope under his chin. Her left hand held it two feet from his halter.

"Walk," she commanded, and stepped out briskly as her right hand urged him to follow suit.

Golden Sovereign obligingly did so for several turns around. By that time his untrained muscles told him a trot would relax him, and he began a mincing gait.

"Walk," Connie barked, emphasizing the command with a steady pressure on the rope. He walked.

Two or three more circuits and she spoke again. "Whoa!" This time the pressure was firm and sudden. Surprise more than anything halted him in his tracks, but she praised him as though he had just stood on his head. Then, reversing hands and directions, they repeated the process.

Once again they took the track in their original manner, but the commands "Whoa" were much more frequent, though never in the same spot as a previous halt. After numerous repetitions, Connie was thrilled to feel Golden Sovereign's pace slacken at the command an instant before her pressure on the rope. She nodded triumphantly toward Pete, who still stood in the center, somewhat glassy-eyed from watching them circle him. In either direction the golden horse began to understand that the voice was something to be obeyed.

After more petting and extravagant praise for his smartness, Connie patiently recommenced trudging around the ring. Her arms maintained the same position, but imperceptibly she began retreating along the rope toward Pete. Now she kept up a running conversation with the horse in order that he would feel her nearness in spite of the foot or two that separated them.

"Whoa!" Back the other way they started, Connie first right beside him but gradually widening the distance between them. Several rounds more, and Connie called the final "Whoa."

"Don't want to get him sick of it almost before we start. Come on in the center, Pete. We'll call it a day while he's acting so lamby."

The rope was carefully recoiled with a minimum of alarm to Golden Sovereign, who returned to his stall. Boy and girl then looked about for further entertainment.

"Pete, let's see how Lady Luck longes! She's had rest enough, and a little easy exercise will do her good."

"Oh boy, Con, let's." Pete assented eagerly. "It'll tell us something about her past, too; for if she has ever been a high-class horse, she ought to have been longed."

They opened the stall door and the lady herself turned to greet them. "Huh-huh-huh," she said.

"Pete, she spoke to us. It's the first time since she came that she's shown any affection for anybody. You're on the mend, old girl," Connie gloated. "Now we're going to take you on another short leg of the road back."

Brush and currycomb were plied vigorously yet gently on the chestnut hide which had begun to lose some of its moth-eaten look. In the short time she had been at McGuire's some of her agonizing thinness had disappeared. Bones were in evidence by the score, but they were thinly covered, whereas the day of her arrival it had seemed that with every movement some point or other would surely pierce the skin.

"I hope she soon grows out that tail you so gaily clipped," Pete complained. "There's no satisfaction in brushing that bony old rattail. Considering what we have to work with, I think you'd call her groomed now." He banged out the brush and comb for emphasis.

The web halter was slipped over her ears and snapped, and the new pupil was ready for her entrance into Shamrock Stables' school. Positions were resumed, and Connie stepped out with Lady Luck on the word, "Walk."

Almost at once she cried, "Whoa." The chestnut mare stopped dead in her tracks.

"Of course, that might just be because she's so worn out," Connie cautioned Pete in an attempt to steady her own hopes.

They reversed, walked, and stopped again like a clock. The girl retreated to the center and again commanded, "Walk." Lady Luck stepped out at the end of her rope as bravely as she could, considering her disabilities, and she was allowed to make several circuits.

"This'll prove it," Connie whispered to Pete. "Trot!"

Obediently the mare swung into her version of a trot. To be sure she was trying, even in soft footing, to limp on all four feet, and her bones practically rattled together from the effort, but still it was a trot. Half a turn was all Connie's heart could stand of the spectacle before she cried, "Walk," and then "Whoa." She was rewarded with an instant response. By tacit agreement the two of them furled in the line and stood by Lady Luck.

"She is—she was—that means," they babbled simultaneously.

"But we've just *got* to find out where and when. And prove it!" Pete asserted.

"Imagine! Trying to find a laundryman in the city who has a name like a breakfast food," Connie exclaimed in exasperation. "Let Bran Flakes do your washing. Does that sound right? No!"

"Connie! The Chamber of Commerce ought to have it. Why didn't I think of that before I came out here. Now it's closed till Monday, and I have to go back to college tomorrow night. Oh me!" Pete thumped his forehead in anguish.

"We could write 'em, Pete, and have the letter come to me. Then the next time you get home we can follow it up—that is, we can if the Chamber of Commerce is good at guessing games."

"You know what, Connie? We ought to have a picture of Lady Luck to show when either of us is asking somebody if they knew her when. Just to say a chestnut mare with a white mark on her forehead and two white feet may not help much."

"Hold her a sec and I'll see if Mom has any exposures left in her camera."

To think was to act with Connie, and she sped off toward the house, to return with Mrs. McGuire's camera. She was about to press the button, but lowered the camera.

"Jiminy. This won't help us much if we ever catch up with whoever owned her when she was a real horse. No one would ever recognize that," she gestured toward Lady Luck who stood dejectedly, head lower than her back and one hindquarter so relaxed a hat could hang on her hip-bone, "as the pride of their stables, I hope!"

"Silly, we can take other pictures as she improves," Pete jeered. "There'll probably be all kinds of time to get her into the pink of condition before we need to worry about her being recognizable to her original owner."

"Sure enough, we can, can't we?" Connie grinned at her hasty speech. She aimed the camera, "Smile, Lady Luck, and maybe lady luck'll smile on you."

Click. Another shot from the mare's off side and the film was rolled up.

"If we write that letter now, so's you can mail it when you go back, the Chamber of Commerce will get it Monday morning. They'll need plenty of time."

McGuire and Kendall, Detectives Extraordinary, went into a business conference on the spot. The letter written to their mutual satisfaction, Pete made moves to leave.

"Don't be downhearted about your plans, Connie. Remember what you told me—it takes time to work some things out." He sounded serious, but behind his eyes there was a glow which encouraged Connie, though she took it to be humor at handing her advice back to her.

"O.K., Grampa. I'll remember what you say," she flung at his retreating back.

CHAPTER FIVE

WHAT BREAKFAST FOOD?

EACH PASSING WEEK CONTRIBUTED some small improvement in Lady Luck's equine beauty. One day Connie noticed that her coat began to have a little shine. Another time she noted that the roached mane and scraggly tail were beginning to fuzz out. Even the stubborn sores were beginning to dry and heal, and her legs lost some of their puffiness. But no further clue had been uncovered linking her present to her past.

Connie had had little time to give to the mare during the intervening weeks, however, since senior-year activities and homework had prevented her from spending much time with the horses. The only reply to their letter to the metropolitan Chamber of Commerce had been a dignified little regret that they had been unable to discover any laundries among those listed which sounded like a breakfast food. Pressure of her other affairs had even cushioned this disappointment.

Always in the back of her mind, there was a nagging wish for her coveted barn and the adjacent farm which would lend itself so perfectly to Shamrock Stable purposes. No matter how she figured, it always totaled up the same: no. March had nearly blown itself out like a lion when Mr. McGuire came stamping into the house from a trip to town, shaking the rain from his coat.

"Connemara, which of the little people are you friendliest with? Put in a good word for me, too. Being your father, I might bask in reflected good luck."

"What d'ya mean, Dad? What's up?" she inquired from her station near the ruddy kitchen range.

"It's a funny thing, and almost makes me believe what you said awhile back," he mused. "Today when I was going past Joe Brand's office he came out and called me back. 'Say, Jim, you still interested in farming the Clinton place on shares?'

"'Sure,' says I, 'if its absent owners wouldn't rather grow a fine crop of weeds instead of the things God intended to feed his own creatures.'"

"Yes, Dad, yes," Connie hurried him hopefully.

"'Well,' he says, 'it's just been sold to some fellow who lives a way off—bought it now to retire to later on, I understand—but he wants it to be cultivated so he won't retire to the best stand of burdock, thistles, and stuff you ever saw. So if you really want to farm it for a few years on a share-the-crop basis, it's yours.'"

"Yippee! Yippee!" Connie made the kitchen

ring with her shrieks of joy. "Now we can build the barn, and it'll be busting with hay and grain upstairs, and busting with horses downstairs. Shamrock Stables, here we come! Did you sign up for it, Dad?" Alarm lest something go awry jerked her back to business methods.

"No, but I will tomorrow. Joe said he'd wait that long before asking anybody else, since he remembered I'd asked about it recently. I just thought I'd make sure you're blowing in the same direction this week that you were awhile ago. I see you are," he smiled.

"Oh yes, Dad, I'm blowing a gale. You'd better get right in there the first thing in the morning so he can't possibly let anybody else have it. Can I go with you?"

"Why not? Might as well meet you there and go talk to a contractor about a barn. Any idea what sort of a one you want?"

"Sure. Got the plans all sketched in my note-book—civics, I think it's under. It's such a lovely barn, and to think I never expected it'd materialize." Connie crowed and crooned to herself as she hurriedly leafed to her dream-barn plans.

"I suppose we're lucky, Mother, that she hasn't a lot of silly ideas, but I do wish Connemara'd be that excited over a new dress," Mr. McGuire lamented, as though his daughter were not present.

"But I don't need a dress. I've got a dress," Connie shot back.

Her parents helplessly lifted their eyes skyward

at her answer, knowing full well that she was past argument or reason on anything which concerned her horses.

"Oh, I hope Pete comes home this weekend. I can hardly wait to tell him. Wonder how long it'll be before he can bring Waltz Dream out to stay? We'll have to get busy and get some boarders lined up too."

"Wait a minute there. The papers haven't even been signed, let alone the barn built and holding hay to feed them. Remember, young lady, there'll be a lot of work for you to do. We'll have to get that new ground plowed up and hay and other crops planted. But Connemara, quiet down while I ask you this. Are you sure you'd rather use your college money for next year and run the risk of not even being able to start a year from this fall? Plenty of things can happen, you know, that would make it impossible for you to go then, but we have the money now. Don't answer me until I've counted ten." Her father and mother solemnly watched her while his hand rose and fell ten times.

"Plenty of things could happen, Dad, but they won't. I'll wait and count on my Irish luck to pull me through next year." Her words sounded careless, but her folks realized that she spoke sincerely and was fully aware of the uncertainties of life.

From that time on Connie's interest in the weather was as personal as the health of a good friend. If it were an early spring, the new crops could be started promptly. If it were a wet, backward season, valuable time would be wasted.

Truly it did seem as though Ireland's little people were on Connie's side, for the first robin was alone but a short time before others joined him, and just a wink after the earliest spring flowers showed, trees were dressing in their new green leaves, fruit trees were budding, and it was spring, and vacation!

Pete's first visit during vacation began jubilantly, and every detail of the barn plans had to be discussed as well as the planting plan for the new land. Once the talk had veered around to Lady Luck, silence fell. They pondered it deeply, but sighs were their only comments.

"Maybe we ought to make a list of breakfast foods, Pete. That might help in checking the city directory," Connie suggested, more to break the dismal silence than from any conviction.

"No good. If one had been listed, the Chamber of Commerce would have caught it."

"It's no good moping anyway. Let's work Golden Sovereign a little. Tomorrow we start plowing and I won't have any time." Connie slid to the ground and went to his stall, Pete behind her. "We might use the bridle today; he ought to be in the whole bitting harness as soon as possible."

Bridles were no novelty to Golden Sovereign, inasmuch as Connie had played and worked with him since he was a baby and she was as familiar to him as his mother, Silver Birch. All his life Connie had handled him, and just about as far back as he could remember she would occasionally slip a piece of leather into his mouth. Curiosity made him mouth it thoughtfully, and it had not been long before it even seemed rather pleasant. Halters were no stranger than his own stall, so a combination of the two—a halter over his head and a round strap through his mouth—was nothing to get excited about. No finesse was needed in handling the lead rope, for since their first session Connie and Golden Sovereign had had many others in the pasture, until he was letter-perfect in his part.

"Walk," she snapped, and the horse who seemed too beautiful to be real stepped out. Around and around he went, walking up smartly without any hesitation.

"Trot." His legs stretched out snappily in a trot which exhibited free action and an even gait.

"Canter." The four white legs rocked into a canter and Connie and Pete in the center of the ring were well-nigh hypnotized by the white feet twinkling back and forth. At this faster pace Golden Sovereign periodically flourished his heels in the air or shook his head to feel the breeze blow through his thick mane and forelock.

"Whoa," Connie crackled suddenly, and he nearly stood on his nose to stop.

"He ought to settle on his haunches more 'stead of throwing the weight on his forequarters," Connie criticized.

"Have a heart," Pete pleaded for the horse. "He isn't even two years old yet, and you want perfection. You know, it's hard to describe his action. He isn't really smooth, but he has all the gangling grace of a schoolboy. Not really clumsy, yet suggesting it; not really graceful, but suggesting that too."

"Pete, you're growing lyrical about him. Tell us more," Connie begged.

"Might go to your heads," the young man shrugged. "Let's see him going on the other track."

Golden Sovereign was reversed, with a pause for petting and praise, since it was impossible at this stage to change his direction by remote control.

"Walk," "Canter," "Trot," came the commands this time to avoid his getting accustomed to a pattern. After the final "Whoa," Connie began to coil the rope.

"He's been so good today, I think we'll put him up now. It's best to do it slowly. Time is the cheapest commodity there is in horse training, and there'll be another day."

"Going to begin plowing tomorrow, eh? Wonder if your father could use a good man?" Pete conjectured. "There's nothing to do at home, and I'd like to harden up some before baseball season starts."

"He might be able to use you," Connie agreed. "Just how straight a furrow do you turn, my good man?"

"Well, mum, my furrows are the artistic kind —curves, not straight lines—but maybe I could help on something else—you know, disking or dragging, any of those other things you do," he explained lamely.

Mr. McGuire himself was consulted and after a keen look at Pete, to make sure he meant it, agreed. "It'll be hard work though, and not very exciting."

"Just what I'm looking for," Pete vowed. "I'll be here early tomorrow in my work clothes."

There followed a week of intense activity. As one day succeeded another, furrow after furrow of the new land was laid bare and broken open to the sun and air to make it ready for the seeds. Even Midnight was put into harness for some of the lighter work, and at the end of the day men and horses were dead tired. After the first day or two, Pete brought his toothbrush and razor with him and bunked there, too.

Connie, of course, was unable to help much with the heavy work and had to be content with helping to care for the horses morning and night, riding out on Silver Birch with a midmorning snack, and doing extra chores. During her odd moments she began to fuss more over Lady Luck, who responded like an orphan child that's been taken into a real home.

"Old girl, I wish you could talk. You look smart enough to. Don't you think if you really tried you could squeeze out either the name of that miserable breakfast food or, better yet, your original owner's name? Come on, one—two—three—what is it?"

"Huh-huh-huh," was all Lady would say, and

that probably because Connie was rustling some grain in her pocket.

"You get ten for trying, but it's not good enough, girlie." Connie slapped her companionably on the shoulder. "Breakfast foods! What breakfast food? Kellogg, Post, Ralston, Cream of Wheat—who ever heard of a Cream of Wheat Laundry?" she disgustedly asked the mare.

"If I'm going to get any action today, I guess Golden Sovereign will have to furnish it. This might be the time to start him in the whole bitting harness," she told herself.

The bitting bridle was gently slipped over his ears and adjusted comfortably, and Connie then approached with the harness. A lightweight back pad with crupper, it had short, adjustable reins which snapped to the bridle rings. In addition there was a check which slipped through a pulley by the ears and fastened to the bits at one end and the back pad at the other. In this manner the horse learned that, however he pulled or worked at the bits, it was himself he was pulling against.

Golden Sovereign had been accustomed many times to having things laid across his back, so they had no trouble there. The crupper, however, might prove to be a different story, and Connie took the precaution of warming and slightly greasing it to prevent the rubber composition from chafing the young colt. Her soothing babble of nonsense continued while she gathered the tail hairs into a knot and gently thrust them through the crupper's loop. Feeling that strange bulky object under his tail, Golden Sovereign tucked it down as tightly as he could and his hindquarters involuntarily bounced in protest.

"Easy, boy, don't let it scare you," she crooned. "I know it feels strange, but it's nothing to get excited about."

She patted him vigorously to distract his attention from the proceedings, and after making certain that the connecting strap was long enough for his back, she settled the back pad into position and with a gently firm motion pulled it snug and fastened it.

Her motions were slow, but each one counted as she snapped the reins to the bridle and adjusted the check long enough so that the young horse's position was only slightly altered from his normal stance. She moved about him, examining straps and buckles to make certain that nothing that could be helped was chafing him.

"We'll just let you stand in that for a few minutes today, laddie. You've been good as gold, and I don't want to aggravate you with it before we really start."

She lounged in the stall to keep him company during his first real lesson. He stood motionless at first, but gradually he began to work against his harness. Strangely enough, when he stuck his nose out, that band around his middle grew terribly tight. If his head sank the littlest bit, he could feel it in his mouth and clear to the roots of his tail where that thing dug into his skin.

Remembering that Connie was still there at one side, he turned his head to see if she could be the one digging into his ribs or hurting his tail, only to discover that when he turned sideways the bit pulled his mouth askew.

Connie burst into laughter at his droll combination of rolling eyes, yawing mouth, and lolling tongue, and his surprised discovery that she was not even near.

"Guess I'd better leave you alone after all to work this out. You've got to understand that it's you doing it to yourself and that I have nothing to do with it."

She stepped into the paddock to visit with Silver Birch and Midnight Moon for a few minutes before she returned to unharness the colt. He shook his head vigorously to lose the feeling of his bondage, and Connie helped by brushing him down.

"Did you grow this beautiful golden coat on purpose, laddie, just so people would love to groom you and make you feel good?" she murmured as the brush slid across his burnished hide. "I almost feel as though I should use metal polish instead of elbow grease on you."

Voices outside the barn told her that she had dallied so late her mother would be looking for help with supper, and she scurried houseward.

CHAPTER SIX

DREAM BARN

SUCH A MIXTURE OF WORK AND PLAY made the vacation days fly, and by the time planting preparations were completed it was Saturday afternoon. The three of them had stabled the horses and were strolling through the yard.

"Connemara, I'm ashamed of you for being such a slave driver. The least you could do is go to the movies with the hired man tonight," Mr. McGuire joshed his daughter, who grew pink at his forwardness in mentioning the very thing she had been thinking.

"Miss McGuire, mum, I'd be honored to have the pleasure of your company," Pete mumbled in mock embarrassment. "How about zipping in to see a double feature?" His pace changed suddenly.

"Why not?" she countered. "You're a very unusual hired man. Bet I'm dressed before you are."

"No fair if you get into the bathroom first," he yelled at her retreating shape, but he took steps, long ones, to see that she didn't.

The days were lengthening, and the two drove along in the soft spring twilight, enjoying it to the utmost. They were practically in the city before wondering where they'd go and what they'd do, but it was pleasant just to ride, so they cruised on leisurely. They came to the center of the city, but it seemed too early to go into a movie and they just kept going. Presently the country lay ahead again.

"Don't let's go on any of the streets we've ever been on before going back," Connie suggested. "Even if you have lived here all your life, there must be lots of streets you've never seen."

In answer Pete flipped the wheel and they turned into a cross street which led to another and another. Once or twice he paused at an intersection, but after a moment's hesitation the car rolled forward. Connie leaned back and relished the feeling of strange places she had never seen before, and unconsciously her eyes darted left and right. Whenever the word LAUNDRY loomed ahead she peered intently at it for an instant before her eyes slid past.

Darkness had almost fallen, and in some stores lights were coming on. Connie blinked at a sign as they drove by a window. She half relaxed, turned again to look at it, and her hand clutched Pete's arm.

"Look, Pete. Do you think—" Her question trailed off as the car stopped and he too stared at the sign. HAND LAUNDRY. SHIRTS, UNIFORMS AND BLOUSES A SPECIALTY. R. R. ALSTON, PROP.

Its shades were drawn, but a light behind them proved someone was working late.

"Let's find out anyway."

Pete knocked on the door but a voice inside called, "We're closed. Too late for new bundles or deliveries. Come back Monday."

"We want to see you about something else," Pete called. "Something important."

"Not something important like a clean shirt for tonight?" a doubting voice cross-questioned.

After further protestations from those outside that the business was neither dirty laundry nor clean laundry, the shade was raised and a wizened old lady peered out. Then the bolt was grudgingly drawn and they stepped inside.

"Could we speak to the owner, please? We'd like to ask him about a horse," Pete explained.

"He's upstairs, but we don't never rent the horse and wagon. Go to a livery stable if you want to get a horse to lark around with," she suggested querulously.

"But it's about one maybe he used to have. Not the one you have now."

Still looking at them with suspicion, the woman

drew back a curtain and shouted, "Paw, c'n you come down here? Somebody wants to talk to you."

Connie listened with mounting excitement to heavy footsteps descending a ramshackle flight of stairs, and her first thought as the man stepped through the curtain was that Lady Luck wouldn't have been much worse off with the junkman.

Pete was the spokesman, and in as few words as possible he told his unsavory host the reason for their call. He admitted to having had several horses, but it was difficult to describe Lady in a fashion that would make this man remember her, for obviously what he considered important they did not. In desperation, Pete turned to Connie.

"The picture—do you have it with you?"

"Oh yes—that is, I think I have." Her heart beating fast, Connie riffled through the papers in her purse and extracted the snapshot.

"That one? Yes, I had her, but she was no good. Got her from a man who had had a riding stable at the lake a year or two ago, and was I gypped! He told me she was a good harness horse, but she couldn't pull nothin'. At first, that is; but I showed her who was boss and wouldn't put up with any of her yellow streak, I did." His lips bit down on the last words and gooseflesh rose on Connie as she pictured the process of learning "who was boss."

"What riding stable was it? Do you remember?" Pete pressed on.

"Lessee—Grogan's? no, or Hogan's? no. Nolan's! That was it. Nolan's. Feller brought his horses every summer from near Detroit. His first name wa-a-as," he hesitated again, "Jim. Or was it George? Something like that anyway."

Simultaneously the two young people decided they had gotten as much real information as they ever would, and backed out.

"Now there's a helpful man if I ever saw one," Pete exclaimed, and launched into a mimic of Mr. R. R. Alston.

"Each time the trail gets a little dimmer," Connie said plaintively. "If it keeps on this way, we'll be looking for a man with two eyes and two ears who lives in Michigan. But we'll find him, or my name isn't Connemara Anastasia McGuire!"

As though in answer to Connie's urgent request, spring was especially nice, and gradually the brown of new-plowed land shaded to light green and then into a deeper, stronger green as the new crops took hold. Mr. McGuire watched the skies suspiciously, expecting to see signs of spring's change of heart so common to northern latitudes, but except for the normal rains the weather was perfection.

One evening in May the three of them stood on the back porch before going in to their evening's occupations—Connie to her homework, and her mother and father to sewing and reading.

"Think it's going to be a nice day tomorrow?" he questioned.

Connie cocked a weather eye skyward, noted

the clear colors in the sunset. "Yes, and the day after that. Why? What's up?"

"Oh, nothing much, but the men are going to begin bringing lumber for the barn. Probably'll begin construction next week. We might walk down there now and agree on just where it's to go in case you aren't here the minute they want to start."

Thenceforth, for weeks Connie was in transports of delight. Each night she raced home from town to see what progress had been made, and when she saw the framework looming against the sky she thought she was as thrilled as she'd ever be. When the roof was on, its shingles almost as golden as Golden Sovereign, she was voluble as a parrot. But when it was at last complete and she and her father walked through it, now quiet and deserted by carpenters, though she shivered with delight, she was wordless.

"You like it, don't you?" her father asked curiously.

"Oh yes. It's beautiful. I'd be willing to give up *two* years of college for it, Dad."

Her eyes traveled along the row of stalls and pictured a handsome, intelligent head thrust over each door, every eye looking at her, Manager of Shamrock Stables.

"I can hardly wait to see a horse in each stall," she fretted.

"Guess I'll have to start calling you Sooner. Here you've no sooner got one thing finished than you're yearning for the next."

Baffled once more by his daughter's single-mindedness, Mr. McGuire departed and left Connie to drift along the row of stalls and in her mind's eye to see them filled with spirited horses, full of life and beauty, but obeying the slightest crook of her little finger.

Going into the home stretch of senior year in high school, Connie decided she just wouldn't have time for a few weeks to exercise the horses properly; and since the weather by then was June at its best, the decision was made to turn them all out to pasture.

Connie led them one by one into the lane and slipped the rope off the shiny satin-smooth neck, whether black or silver or chestnut, and each one seemed to know that it was more than just an afternoon's outing. As though they were playing Follow the Leader, each in turn kicked off a few paces, dropped to her knees, and rolled over for a good back scratching, then regained her feet and turned to look at the girl. When all three were grouped a little way off, Connie waved the rope at them.

"Go on, girls. Go on back into the woods and vegetate. While I've got the knowledge of centuries on my mind, I've no time for the likes of you. But do I envy you!"

She returned to the stable and three pairs of eyes switched to the other corner of the barn as that door opened and Connie led Golden Sovereign out into the sunlight.

" 'S too bad you have to play by yourself, fellow, but you have a nice pasture all your own to frolic in. Pity poor me who has to grow old and stoop-shouldered over the Elizabethan drama, or would you prefer American history?"

Connie's hand slid reluctantly from his head along the burnished neck and shoulders across barrel and flank until he realized that he was free. With a hop and a skip he leaped into freedom, and though his caperings resembled those of the mares, there was more and better of everything with a few additions of his own, such as side skips and rearing. He polished it all off with a vigorous roll and regained his feet. The group of admiring mares in the adjoining lane snared his interest, and with head high he swept over to pay his compliments.

Her eye followed them as they drifted along, the mares in the lane and Golden Sovereign curving his neck over the intervening fence, nickering to them, until he came to the corner of his pasture. From that barrier he had to watch the others disappear from sight at the turn of the lane.

Connie returned to the barn to hang the rope on its peg and started for the house, where she descended into a maelstrom of feverish cramming for final examinations. Several nights she stayed in town with Di in order that they might pool their knowledge and thereby assist each other to hang the proper information on its right mental peg.

Their combined efforts were successful, for

many days later when Connie reappeared at home only the graduation ceremony and some evening festivity separated her from having finished what schooling Tyrone had to offer. Her sadness at having closed one chapter of her life was mingled with joy at the prospect of the days and weeks ahead when she could work uninterrupted with her horses. Even her friends' discussion of colleges and curriculums could not dampen her enthusiasm for the months that stretched before her.

Connie delayed going to her horses only as long as it took to change into old clothes. The barn, when she stepped in for a rope, was dark and silent without her well-loved friends there, and she hurried on toward the woods, stopping only to tell her father in a neighboring field that it was all over but the diploma.

She pursed her lips in the old familiar whistle with which she had wooed and won Silver Birch several years before. Deep in the woods she heard the answering neigh, so she sauntered happily in that direction. Again she whistled, and the answer was closer. Soon she heard leaves rustling at the tramping of hoofs, and as she approached a clearing from one side the horses stepped into it from the other.

Again she whistled, but this time in surprise. Not three, but four horses faced her! Golden Sovereign, every inch a king, minced forward to investigate, ears flicking back and forth, nostrils fluttering nervously.

"Hello there, you old ladies' man. How in the world did you get out here? And how am I going to get all of you back to the barn? I'm surely not going to try to ride Silver with you looking after her so jealousy."

She circled them and then, waving her arms and tossing bits of bark, she started them toward the lane to the barn. When they showed signs of slowing up, she threw back her head and gave what she fondly believed to be a wolf call, followed by a bobcat's and any other wild animal's she could aspire to imitate.

Mr. McGuire, attracted by Connie's vocal activities, was standing by the fence in his field to see what was going on when Connie, preceded by the horses, emerged from the woods.

"Well, I'll be—I'll be jiggered. He must have jumped the fence, but I wonder when. He was there yesterday—I think. Or was it day before yesterday? Or when—?" He hesitated.

"Do you think he hurt himself jumping that fence, Dad? D'ya see any marks on him?" Connie anxiously asked.

"No, I don't. But I guess we're going to have a crop of foals before we'd expected to. Look at him there, circling them and guarding them as if they were his band of wild mares and he was king of the prairie."

Connie was startled at this turn of events, but not for long. The prospect of three foals—all like Golden Sovereign, of course—erased her fears for his possible injury in this escapade. Not until all four of them had been shut up in their respective stalls did she have time to consider the glorious future.

"My goodness, how'll I ever be able to wait until next May to see them?" she asked herself. "Golden Sovereign," she addressed him. "We've got some busy days ahead so that you'll be a credit to your babies when they're born. The better you are, the better that'll make them, and that's got to be pretty wonderful!"

CHAPTER SEVEN

HORSY HANDS

To SAVOR HER NEW FREEDOM the day after Commencement, Connie decided to ride over to the lake and talk with Dr. Casey of the Laughing Horse Stables. The years turned back for her as she saddled Silver Birch and started out. She noted June present in every tree and bush and bird, but presently was content to soak it up through her pores while her mind reverted to the evening before.

"The man told us, Silver, that we should strive to live our lives so that when we die the world will be just a little bit better than we'd found it. That might be by inventing some wonderful new machine, or discovering a marvelous medicine, or maybe just being so happy and pleasant that people feel better for having known us."

Silver's hoofs ticked off several seconds while Connie reconsidered her words.

"Would raising good horses for people to love and enjoy make the world better? It'd make the

horses better and, yes, I think that people can't
help being better if they love horses and ride
them days like this."

Satisfied that she would be doing her part in
the scheme of things, Connie touched Silver into
a canter and they rocked along rhythmically. Her
hand strayed to the foam of tossing mane as she
thought of the happy and sad days she had
known with this darling of her heart.

From habit, Silver turned into the Laughing
Horse gate. At the sound of hoofs, Dr. Casey
thrust his head out of the office door and then
hurried to greet a fellow horseman.

"Hello, Connemara. What's on your mind—or
is this purely a social call?"

"I guess it's a little of both, Doc. Did you ever
hear of a riding-stable man around here named
Jim or George Grogan or Hogan or Nolan?"

"What is this, the prelude to an Irish joke?" he
jovially countered. On noting Connie's serious mien he paused to consider. "Nolan, eh?
No-o-o, can't say as I have, but that doesn't mean
anything. I'm awful at names. Why, does he owe
you money?"

"No, I'd just like to locate him, that's all," Connie parried. "Let me know if it should come to
you later, will you?"

Connie had looked over all the new horses at
the stables, given a friendly pat to those she already knew, and the two of them were relaxing
on the office porch over bottles of soft drinks
when Pete's car drove up.

"Look who's here!" Dr. Casey exclaimed. "My stableboy emeritus no less. All through college for awhile, Pete?"

"Yeah, they had to close the place to finally get me out," the redhead quipped. "Has Connie been telling you about the latest McGuire madness?"

Dr. Casey wheeled on Connie. "Are you holding out on me? And after all you've taught me," he smiled. "What's up now?"

In alternate sentences Connie and Pete detailed Lady Luck's advent and what they knew of her past.

"So you just wondered if I'd ever heard of a Jim or George Grogan or Hogan or Nolan? I still haven't, but I'll certainly see what I can find out." His eyes grew thoughtful.

"I'm sorry for not telling you, Doc. But I've taken so much joking about her I guess I've grown too cautious. Pete is the only one who agrees with me, but you should see her, Doc. I'll bet you'd recognize faded gentility when you saw it."

"If you see it, it's good enough for me, Connemara. Real horsemen are born, and I'd stake a golden horseshoe to a rubber one that one of your great-grandpappies was chief equerry at Tara itself in the days when its harps were playing."

To Dr. Casey's sincere tribute, Pete added, "You know, for people who can make things grow there's the saying that they have a green hand —or is it a thumb? Anyway, I think Connie has a horsy hand, for she can certainly do things with horses no one else can."

"My hands always smell horsy, if that's what you mean," she laughed deprecatingly. "Say, Doc, I almost forgot part of my business. If you hear of anyone who wants to board their horse, send 'em to me, will you? I'm going to stick around home next year and I'd like to pick up a little extra money. We'll take horses either for straight board or with special arrangements for paddock exercise or, if they want, I'll ride or train them myself. Come one, come all, I hope," she intoned prayerfully.

"Likely I can help, Connemara; people often do ask me to recommend a place, and I can deflect the overflow from my stables to yours. But just from idle curiosity, where're you going to put them—unless your barn has elastic walls?"

In glowing terms Connie described the new barn and her budding plans. Doc whistled long and shrill. "Looks like I'll just have to drop in one day soon and see all these improvements. I'd better watch out or you'll have the Laughing Horse Stables backed right off the map."

"Oh no, Doc," Connie seriously replied. "We're in different divisions of the same business."

The next morning when Connie walked toward the barn she felt like a new person. Instead of having to fit her horse training into spare time, and often having to forego or postpone an important bit, the days and weeks and months stretched before her invitingly. Nothing else to do, nothing else to worry about but just what went on at the farm.

She moved along the stalls, rubbing an inquisitive nose or tweaking a foretop, but it was at Golden Sovereign's stall she stopped. He had watched her progress, and now, as though in greeting, he nodded his head vigorously over the door. Her finger traced the white strip down his face, and while tousling his foretop she gave a few satisfying little digs around the ears.

"I'd get more done with you, my man, if I didn't take up so much time admiring you. But you'll never learn manners that way."

She forthwith got the bitting harness and buckled him into it. After letting him stand in it just a few minutes, they went into the paddock for the real lesson, and Golden Sovereign walked along smartly at his end of the rope. He trotted, cantered, walked, cantered, trotted, walked in succession as she called the pace, and her critical eye could find no flaw.

In contrast to his first gangling gaits, he looked as stylish as a circus horse—his neck was crisply arched, his hoofs flung themselves forward like pendulums at the trot, and while cantering his gait was so smooth it seemed that a glass of water on his back wouldn't spill a drop.

"Maybe I'd better get a plume for your bridle and a ruffled skirt for me and go into the bareback business," she told him during a breather. "You're getting so good at this, it's high time we went on to the next lesson."

One end of the rope was slipped through the ring on the back pad and snapped onto the bit. The long end was brought around in back, slipped through the other back-pad ring, and fastened to the bit. Standing still, she moved them around gently, sometimes touching his sides or back until he became accustomed to this new feeling. Never did she allow them to get snarled into his tail which switched nervously.

When he no longer flinched at the rope's touch, nor started in surprise, Connie cried, "Walk," and they followed the path already worn by his circling hoofs. Her arms were stretched up and wide apart to prevent their motion from slapping him with the rope, but her touch on the reins was feather soft. The two gained confidence together before a gentle pressure on one rein swung Golden Sovereign away from his path. At first he was confused at finding himself off familiar ground and halted. Her softly determined voice sent him on again, and the other rein inclined him in the opposite direction.

So they angled around the paddock, her hands telegraphing her directions to him, and though there were occasional misunderstandings, these were soon corrected. A few minutes were all Connie gave him of this work.

"Time's up, mannie. You're almost too good to be true so far." Her voice petted him as much as her hands, and his brown eyes seemed to sparkle with pride, but she realized it was just his normally bright look.

The next day and the next day and the next day Connie and Golden Sovereign rehearsed their lessons in the paddock, and he was so quick to understand what she wanted she was tempted to cut corners in the training. No sooner had the temptation arisen than the girl quashed it firmly, knowing well that an hour or a day saved at that stage might require a month or a year later to unlearn bad habits.

When Connie and her folks returned from church the following Sunday, they found Pete lounging on the porch, his feet on the railing. Mr. and Mrs. McGuire's love for Connemara was something quite apart from their disappointment at having no son, and they welcomed Pete's visits, whether heralded or not. He was urged to eat dinner with them.

"Eat hearty, Connie, you'll need it this afternoon." At her startled look Pete continued, "We're going to ride around the lake today. You were going to invite your guest for a horseback ride, weren't you?" he questioned plaintively.

"Looks like I don't need to. You were going to ask me to come along then," she countered. "Why this sudden ambition to ride around the lake?"

"It's a nice day, for one thing, and I thought it'd be nice to drop in at *the other stables* for a visit—just to show them that we Laughing Horsers are their friends."

Pete heavily accented "the other stables," but not until his left eyelid twitched did Connie catch on that further sleuthing was the order of the day. This sent her scuttling to change, and the empty chicken platter was hardly cool before Silver and Midnight jogged out of the yard, their riders eagerly sniffing the day's promise.

Their first approach was elaborately casual, but as one stable after another yielded no clue, their dialogue simmered down to a few lines.

"D'ya ever hear of a Jim or George Nolan? Or Grogan or Hogan?"

"Does this horse look familiar, or would she if she had more flesh on her bones?"

"Thank you. Could you tell us where the next stable is?"

Though they stopped to investigate at every building large enough to stable two horses, though the snapshot of Lady Luck was passed from hand to hand that day, they were no wiser when the horses jogged into the yard hours later. Silver and Midnight unsaddled and rubbed down, Connie and Pete watched from the top fence rail while they completed their own grooming in a sandy spot.

"Old R. R. Alston must have been having noises in his head if he thought he bought Lady Luck from a stable at the lake," Pete growled. "It's a cinch we didn't miss any."

"Stables or lakes?" Connie murmured idly. "Pete!" she shrieked. "He didn't say which lake. There're a dozen around here, and at least half of 'em have some sort of stable. Maybe that's the answer."

"Oh, are you the brain! Of course that's it. But now—which lake?"

They stared at each other, dismayed at having solved one problem only to be confronted by a larger one. Pete broke the silence first.

"Just as sure as we begin guessing hit or miss, we'll pick the right one last. Let's just list the lakes alphabetically and start through them. Some that are near each other we can do all at once; others we'll have to do one at a time. Any better ideas?"

"None at all. Have you got a pencil?"

They squatted on the grass near the barn and hastily jotted down names as their thoughts ranged the county.

"The pioneers who settled this section were matter-of-fact enough when they named things," Pete commented, looking at the list which included Round Lake, Walnut, Pine, Silver, Grass, and other descriptive names.

"It'll take us as long to cover the territory as it took them in an oxcart," Connie rued.

"No, the advantage of transportation will be ours anyway. In my stylish little Asthma we can whisk around them in no time, I hope," Pete promised. "When do we start?"

"It's too late today, I'm afraid. How about to-morrow afternoon? Can you come out then—or any afternoon this week?"

"Your horses, my dear young lady! Have you forgotten your obligations to them in the frenzy of the chase?"

"Oh, I can work them in the morning. And this is for their good, too. The better we can make Lady Luck look, the better for her and the stables. See?" She airily dismissed their claims to her undivided attention.

CHAPTER EIGHT

GOOD AS GOLD

THE DAYS THAT FOLLOWED fell into a pattern: work Golden Sovereign and the other horses each morning, change and drive away with Pete each afternoon. The first day she had started out full of excitement, but returned somewhat crestfallen at their lack of success; and though each time she felt that they were just on the verge of locating Mr. Grogan-Hogan-Nolan, each night they returned empty-handed.

Summer was at its best and any riding stable that ever was open would certainly be in business by then, but at all of them the story was the same. One day they had been at it extra long and the sun was nearly setting before Pete turned the car for the long trip back. Conversation was limited to monosyllables as each sought a solution of their problem.

Two riders on well-lathered horses turned into the road ahead of them from a side road. The car was sliding past when Connie impulsively yelled,

"Where'd you get the horses from?"

"Nolan's Stables," one negligently replied. "They aren't much good though. Wouldn't recommend them."

Tires skidded in gravel at Pete's sudden braking. "Where?" he and Connie demanded in one breath.

"Little Twin Lake," the rider obliged, with an astonished look at such vehemence.

"Thanks a lot," Connie flung back as gravel spurted from under the tires.

"We didn't even have Little Twin on our list, did we, Pete?"

"No, on account of we thought that Big Twin would be the only place where a stable could be. It must be a high-powered establishment, like fun!"

Their destination was several miles away, and in order to get there before dark Pete concentrated on his driving while Connie sat beside him, a tense bundle of anticipation.

"Maybe this is the end. Maybe this man knows where Lady Luck came from and we can track her down. Won't we have the laugh on the others who couldn't tell a good horse in disguise!"

"Don't get too hopeful, Con. If she started out as a good horse, there must have been many owners between then and the shape you found her in," Pete warned matter-of-factly.

Once at Little Twin Lake, it wasn't hard to locate the stable, for there were very few cottages. They piled out of the car and hurried across the yard toward the only visible person.

"Are you Mr. Nolan? We'd like to talk to you about a horse—"

"Nolan isn't here any more, and it's too late to rent horses tonight."

The brisk interruption caught them off balance, and two jaws dropped as one when his words sank in. Connie pulled herself together first.

"But the sign says Nolan's Stables. We wanted to ask about a mare he used to own. Maybe you'd remember her—dark chestnut with a white star on her forehead and two white feet? Any idea where she came from?"

"I bought the place from Nolan last year, and he agreed to let me use the same name—if that's any advantage. Don't remember any such mare since I've been here, and I'm not sure he would. They don't last long between the summer riders here and winters in the city."

"Where is he now? We'd certainly like to talk with him." Pete by now had taken up the slack in his jaw and entered the conversation.

"We-e-ll, I don't rightly know. Seems as though somebody said he was in Detroit working in a factory. I might still have his old address here, if you want to wait a minute."

They eagerly assented and stood around hopefully while the proprietor thumbed through bundles of old letters, bills, and advertisements which seemed to have accumulated through the ages.

"Yeah, here's a letter from him." They pounced delightedly. "But it doesn't have a return address on it."

They drooped.

"Here we are, letter and address and everything. You can have the envelope if you want, but remember it's almost a year and a half old. He mightn't be there now."

After eagerly scanning the worn, dusty envelope it was tucked safely away, and with suitable thanks Pete turned toward the car and Connie followed. Pete wheeled suddenly at the gate.

"Hey," he yelled at the man, "what does G. J. stand for?"

"George Joseph," the man's voice answered through the gathering dusk.

"That's just fine," Connie muttered. "There probably aren't more than two dozen George Joseph Nolans in Detroit. Nothing to it!"

A letter enclosing photographs was the first thing to try, McGuire and Kendall, Detectives Extraordinary, decided, and it was written before Pete left that evening. Had it not been for her horses and work, Connemara would have found the days that followed difficult to endure, but there was always something to claim her attention.

Golden Sovereign was coming along so well in his education that Connie, if she had not known better, would have thought he had already been broken. His footwork progressed so rapidly that she guided him at will all over the pasture at a walk or trot, and many a lesson she finished red-faced and panting from keeping up behind his long-legged trot.

Forward was not the only direction he learned, however, for every well-schooled horse must know how to back. For this, Connie drew in Pete or her father to stand at the stallion's head and push backward on his nose or lightly tap his chest with a whip. She simultaneously vibrated the reins and pulled gently while barking peremptorily, "Back! Back!"

Under their combined pressure the sweet-tempered horse could do nothing else. Though at first he responded grudgingly with only a step or two, after frequent repetition of the lesson Golden Sovereign would continue backing until the "Whoa" command halted him.

Wherever she worked, Connie kept an eye out for the mailman, and he had never driven far off before she was at the mailbox, examining its contents. As day after day went by, her disappointment grew deeper, though she tried to tell herself that delay was better than having the letter returned marked "Unknown."

"The longer it takes, the more addresses it's following him to," she told herself with great firmness. "And he may not answer the minute he receives it either."

Her logic was at last rewarded. In the box was a letter for her in a strange handwriting. She ripped it open and unfolded the letter in one motion.

Dear Miss McGuire:

Sorry to have taken so long to answer your letter which followed me here to Toledo. I do remember the mare you ask about. Had her two or three years. Don't know how much help it will be to tell you I bought her from a livestock jobber whose headquarters were near Grand Rapids, the Western Michigan Livestock Co. She didn't hold up well, and I'm surprised she's lasted as long as this. She was always too willing, no matter how unreasonable her rider, but the man I sold her to said she'd have very little to do. [Connie snorted as the cruel face of R. R. Alston flashed into her mind.] Let me know if I can be of any more help to you.

Yours truly,
G. J. NOLAN

"Here we go again," Connie warned herself. "But the colder and fainter the trail gets, the more determined I am to reach the end. She isn't Lady Luck for nothing."

Pete phoned that evening and Connie relayed the news, but his eager suggestion that they head for Grand Rapids the next day had to be reluctantly declined.

"Can't tomorrow, Pete. Haying starts, and every spear counts this year. When it's over, though, the bubonic plague itself couldn't keep me away from Grand Rapids.

"And Pete, if you don't want to do it, just say so, but Dad asked me to ask you if you'd like to be a hired hand during the haying. He says that you've already done so much work here you shouldn't come unless you're paid. Want to?"

Pete's gay voice zipped back to her across the miles. "I'll make a counterproposal. Let me bring Waltz Dream out to board, and whatever your dad'd pay me can be applied to her account. You'll have hay enough now—or will have soon —and she's entitled to a little summer outing too. Is it a deal?"

Connie turned aside to confer with her father, and arrangements were completed. Haying operations were delayed the next day until Waltz Dream was led, with suitable ceremony, into the new barn and established in a box stall. Connie nearly popped with joy at this first step toward complete fulfillment of her dream, but further gloating was cut short by Mr. McGuire, who whistled them out to the fields with him.

Before setting the mowing machine into the luxuriant stand of hay, he cast one more appraising look at the sky. He tested the wind with his finger and, nodding to himself, directed the chattering blades to cut a swath in the waving spears. Of all the farm work Connemara enjoyed haying the most, not only for its fragrance but because of the sun and wind that marked haying weather and the thick mows of hay that grew deeper and deeper, promise of well-fed horses during the winter.

By the time they finished mowing all the hay, the first field had cured and could be raked, so that the three of them were kept on the jump. During a lull in operations Connie stood in the middle of the new barn floor, snuffing contentedly, when Pete rounded the corner and entered.

"Now if you don't look like an Irish setter with her nose in the wind," he laughed. "Any minute I expect you'll break into a point."

"Um-m-m. Doesn't it smell wonderful, Pete? I love the smell of new lumber any time, and of hay too, but the two together would be worth fifty dollars a dram bottled. Um-m-m," she continued ecstatically.

"Does smell pretty topnotch," he agreed. "And Dad wonders why I'd rather work on a farm than in one of his factories during vacation. Um-m-m," he chorused.

Toward the end of their job, a dark day delayed the hay's curing fast enough to keep pace with them, and Mr. McGuire gave them the day off. Before Connemara felt she could leave, Golden Sovereign must have his lesson. Instead of the back pad from the bitting harness, she substituted that part from a regular buggy harness, but it seemed to make no difference at all to his highness.

"He ought to get used to other hands than mine,

Pete. Want to take him around? You hold the reins and I'll walk beside you and call the commands, so he won't have too many strange things all at once."

Delightedly Pete took the proffered reins, yet even with Connie's voice as an accompaniment, Golden Sovereign turned his head at the strange feel of the reins. Satisfied, he stepped forward. Horse and driver felt each other out for a time, and though the horse knew that different hands held the reins, they were equally light and steady.

More than satisfied for his part, Pete turned to Connie. "Why, his mouth is as soft as silk. He's so responsive to just a heavy breath on one rein, I'll bet you could drive him with silk thread— like in the National Horse Show."

"I'll hardly try it right away, but I'm determined that his mouth will never harden as long as I'm Connemara McGuire."

"You won't be that forever, you know," Pete said slyly, "so we'll hope his mouth stays soft anyway."

"Trot," Connie crackled, and the pink of her face could soon be blamed on the increased pace. Before long, the two of them, but not Golden Sovereign, were huffing and puffing and they dropped back to a walk. Their attention was drawn from the horse by a hail from the barn.

"Hey there, what is this, follow the leader? Or have I let you kids off so easy you have to play fox and geese with a horse?"

The threesome walked over to the fence where

Mr. McGuire leaned, intently watching the proceedings. So much of Connie's work with Golden Sovereign had been at odd times when her father was not around that he was amazed to see the progress she had made.

They admired and discussed the stallion before Connie declared, "He's ready for it; are you two?"

"Ready for what?"

"To be hitched to the cart," she continued. "Right at first I think it'd better be a three-man job: one to stand at his head, and one on each side to hitch up."

Her helpers blinked at her matter-of-fact approach to so epochal an undertaking, but declared themselves ready. The rest of the harness was brought, and slowly and carefully added to what Golden Sovereign already wore. This much Connie had rehearsed him in privately, and he seemed as interested as one of them. His head turned from side to side to stare at the proceedings.

The critical moment of putting horse to cart arrived. Pete held him with a neck rope slipped through the bit, and Mr. McGuire and Connie pulled the two-wheeled cart up behind him, the shafts high over his back. They patted his rump to distract his attention from the stiff poles which were slipped through the loops on each side.

"Hitch him on as long a trace as you can, Connemara. Don't want the cart kicked to pieces the first day," her father advised.

Almost before Golden Sovereign sensed the dif-

ference, his traces had been fastened, the hold-
backs adjusted, and horse and cart were one. Connie joined Pete by the stallion's head and praised
him for his good sense. He stood stock-still briefly.
Then he tossed his head to drive off a fly and, in
the motion, saw that thing directly behind him. A
nervous convulsion ran over him, after which he
stood quivering until their renewed cajolery diverted his thoughts.

"If one of you will walk on each side, about
by his ribs, I'll lead him around for a minute or
two. You'll screen the cart from him a little and
help kill some of its rattle while he gets gradually
accustomed to it."

This phase passed without incident and, em-
boldened, Connie decided to go on to the next
part.

"He might just as well get used to it all at
once. Hold him, you two, while I sneak into the
cart, and he won't notice the added weight much."

One held Golden Sovereign by the bit, the
other handed Connie the reins, and she was on
her own! She kept up a constant patter of conversation to encourage him, and though for all
Golden Sovereign knew or cared she could have
been reciting the Gettysburg Address, his ears
turned back in attention. They circled the field
several times and he was as good as he was gold.
Once a twig caught in the spokes and he leaped
with fright, but his telegraph lines to Connie held
gentle and true, and his confidence in her returned to calm him.

She drove back to where Pete and her father watched in fascination, and Golden Sovereign was carefully unhitched and returned to his stall.

"Isn't he good though," Connie marveled. "He seems as smart as an old horse. If he keeps on this way, it'll be a cinch to train him."

"Just take it up with your little people, Connemara. Your word seems to carry considerable weight with them," her father smilingly advised.

CHAPTER NINE

CAMELLIA OF SUNLIT ACRES

HAYING OPERATIONS RESUMED the next day, and almost before they realized it the first cutting was stowed safely in the barn. Pete departed reluctantly for the city, promising everyone—probably himself more than the McGuires—that he would soon be back to ride Waltz Dream oftener than haying had permitted.

Early the next morning—early even for the first-rooster-crow McGuires—the phone rang, and it was Pete asking to speak to Connie.

"Hello, Con. Great luck. Dad's leaving for a business trip to Grand Rapids now—yeah, in about ten minutes, so I'm going along, and while he's talking cars I'll slip away and talk horses with the Western Michigan Livestock people. We'll be gone several days, so you'd better turn Dreamy into pasture for a fling."

Pete chuckled. "Poor Dad, he thinks I've suddenly developed an interest in the business and want to go for that reason. Suppose I'll have to sit in on one or two powwows, though I'd rather be listening to discussions of martingales and Pelhams than differentials and carburetors. 'By now, I'll be seeing you."

Connie was half glad and half disappointed. Her plans for continuing with Golden Sovereign's driving lessons would be curtailed, for it would be impossible for her father to be around to help each day when the horse had to be hitched up. She pondered her difficulty while she did the morning work, but saw no alternative to volunteering to help with her father's work, in order that he might spare her the necessary time.

Accordingly, after Golden Sovereign had had his trial spin on the longe line, Mr. McGuire was on hand as assistant handler. Each time he had been hitched to the cart, Connie had lengthened the lesson, and the stallion's abundant vitality seemed to rejoice in the added work. Once he had been hitched up, Connie guided him gaily around the pasture.

But for the unstylish breaking cart, they might have been captioned "The Well-turned-out Horse and Driver." Connie sat squarely on the seat, her shoulders back and arms forward as she gripped the reins with delicate strength. Golden Sovereign gleamed like clean sand, and his muscles alternately swelled and smoothed under the skin. Apart from his innate beauty, Connie rejoiced at the improvement in his action, for he was no longer the awkward youth of a few months before, and his legs flashed back and forth with style and dash. His build too had changed, and instead of the thinness of adolescence, he was pounds heavier than he had been but a short time before.

They had flashed around the enclosure so many times Connie felt like a squirrel in a cage. They had crisscrossed and circled at each gait. They had backed and turned until Connie had no more novelty left.

She halted Golden Sovereign by the gate and called, "Hi, Dad. Come open the gate for us, will you? I think I'll take him out on the road. I'll cut into the old road just a little above anyway."

Mr. McGuire looked doubtfully at his daughter in the tiny cart behind the powerful stallion, but reflecting that there was little traffic on the road at that time of day, he acquiesced.

"Take it easy now, Connemara. You know you've got a lot of horsepower there in front of you, and no brakes unless he puts 'em on."

"I will, Dad. Don't worry, but he'll never learn anything as long as we have to go in a circle. 'By."

Golden Sovereign walked sedately down the driveway and into the highroad. Oblivious to the beauties of the morning, Connie kept her mind on her work, and by anticipating possible pitfalls she talked him past them. Once into the old road, where Golden Sovereign trod on grass between the two tracks, she sent him on at a fast trot. Still her hands were soft to his mouth, but there was strength enough to support him as he beat out a rhythmic tune with his hoofs.

At the end of the stretch they wheeled around carefully and came back at a slower, more collected trot. His knees went higher, his neck arched rather than stretched, and with ears set forward every movement he made shouted, "Look at me and admire Golden Sovereign, king of horses, beauty of beauties!"

An advantage of driving instead of riding is that the whole horse is in sight to watch and admire, and Connie drank in every bit. Whether Golden Sovereign was fired by bright sunlight, flecked with sunshine and shade, or glowing with a restrained fire in deep shade, she marveled that a childish determination to have her own horse should bring her to this.

Golden Sovereign was still on tiptoe when she turned him back toward the farm, but he jogged along obediently at a pace which cooled him out in time. In spite of her admonitions not to worry, Connie noted that first her mother's and then her father's head peeked out at the sound of hoofbeats. Their expressions puzzled her briefly.

"Connemara, what do you think happened while you were gone? We accepted our second boarder!"

"You did! What's it like? Oh, I can hardly wait to see it. Where?" Only her handful of horse prevented her from a headlong rush to the stable.

"I've put the boarder next to Golden Sovereign and moved all the mares into the new barn. It'll be easier to take care of 'em all together, and Waltz Dream won't be so lonesome," Mr. McGuire explained while he was helping to unhitch. Connie's eyes darted to the next stall before Golden Sovereign was in his, but she cried out in disappointment,

"You're joking! There's nothing in there."

"Yes, there is, Connemara. Look a little closer," her mother, who had followed them to the barn, advised.

So important a task as grooming the stallion didn't stop Connie from leaving him to peer over the door of the adjoining stall. "A goat! You took in a smelly old goat to live next to Golden Sovereign?" she exclaimed with horror.

"Lady goats don't smell as much as a dog, and this is a lady goat. She's a French Alpine chamoisée, the lady said. Isn't she pretty?" her parents recited.

And she was, pretty as a deer. A soft gray coat, with black accents on her face and legs, was combined with an alert grace. She directed a soft little bleat of greeting at Connie, who continued to hang over the door in astonishment.

"She doesn't seem so bad. What's her name?"

"Camellia of Sunlit Acres. Cows' milk doesn't seem to do anything for you, so we thought maybe goat's milk would fatten you out of the flyweight division. Her owner was going away for a trip and wanted to leave her here. Dr. Casey sent her."

Mollified to hear that Doc had done it, Connie waived the insult to Golden Sovereign and softened enough to stroke the doe's neck. Camellia responded by rubbing her head against the friendly arm.

Golden Sovereign was greatly intrigued by his new neighbor, and they could hear his nostrils at a large crack, snuffing noisily for more information. Camellia's curiosity was accordingly aroused and, standing on her hind legs, she in turn investigated. Nose to nose, horse and goat made each other's acquaintance. Golden Sovereign's lips nibbled tentatively in a caress, and Connie was delighted to see that the two had made friends so easily.

There was no word from Pete the next day nor the next, and Connie perforce had to continue her routine. Golden Sovereign seemed to relish their short trips on the highway and along the old road, but his lessons in the field were not omitted, since the broader area perfected his reining better than merely following a straight course.

At last, when her patience and endurance were almost gone, Pete drove in.

"Didn't mean to be gone so long, but I guess Dad thought that once he had me he'd make the most of it."

Connie impatiently brushed aside his preliminaries. "What luck'd you have, Pete? Did you get all the dope on Lady Luck?"

"Lady Luck? Who's that?" he teased, but relented. "Yes, I did, but I had a dickens of a time. First time I talked with the man, he didn't have any remembrance of her at all. I showed him the snaps, but no soap. After talking myself deaf, dumb, and blind, I left. I was about ready to drive back here and get Lady herself as Exhibit A.

"Then back at the hotel, I got to thinking I ought to try again. So the next day I went out. Same story. Pictures rang no bell, description ditto, so I asked him whether maybe there could be anyone else who might have known the horse better than he did. With that, he called for their stable manager—the man who takes care of the stock while it's waiting to be sold.

"You should have been there. A little old Irishman came stamping in, and I went through my song and dance again. By that time I didn't have much faith in the snaps, and what really did the trick was mentioning the bracelet scar on her left hind leg. You should have seen his face light up. 'Shure and you mean My Lady. Do I remember that little mare! She was the darling of my heart, and if my grandson hadn't been after needing an operation soon I'd have bought her myself. You remember that vanload we sent to Detroit for the sale, Boss,' he said to the owner. 'She was in that lot.'"

"Shure and it takes an Irishman to pick a horse," Connie mimicked. "Then what?"

"'That's fine and dandy, Pat,' I said, 'but where'd she come from? That's what I want to find out.'

"He scratched his head puzzledly, saying, 'Don't hurry me. Don't hurry me,' though neither of us was saying a word. He mumbled to himself, shook his head, mumbled some more. Then his face lighted up like a jack-o'-lantern. 'A man brought her in a trailer, seems like—yes, I recollect now, he had a long scar across his right cheek from temple to chin—not deep, but it looked like a chalk mark across his face.'"

Pete's voice still echoed his disappointment at meeting such a dead end.

" 'I suppose you pay cash for such an on-the-spot transaction, sir?' I questioned the owner of the place.

" 'Yes,' he said, 'at least a guaranteed check,' and zowie! did my hopes rise."

Connie's rapt attention would have been merited by an Academy Award thriller as, with round eyes and parted lips, she listened to Pete's recital. "Go on, go on!" she urged.

" 'Mightn't the old check stub show something then? I'd be glad to reimburse you for any time or trouble it takes to find it. It means a lot to me,' I told them. Well, after a lot of talk about when it was—the old man called his daughter to find out just when his grandson had his leg operated on—we backtracked from there and found the right stub!" Pete paused for breath—and effect.

"I'll jab you with a pitchfork if you don't stop stopping right in the worst places," Connie threatened him fiercely. "Go on!"

"I felt as though I were waiting for Bank Night drawing at the movies as the man cleared his throat and read off the amount for one chestnut mare with white star and two white feet delivered by trailer. Then he stopped, and I thought I'd burst with suspense before he continued. 'Mail check to A. N. Miller, 23 Elm Street, Powell, Michigan.'

" 'So Chalk couldn't have been the real owner,' I began, but paused. The man looked at me a minute and said, 'That seems to be the information you want, and since you offered to pay me, my charge is this: just what in thunder are you so anxious to find out for?' I told him about you and Lady, and what we think about her. He laughed, but the old man nodded his head and said, 'She had royal breeding some place in her past. And I wish ye luck in finding out where.' And tomorrow night if all you kiddies are good, I'll tell you about—" Pete concluded, imitating a radio announcer.

"Go on with you, you exhibitionist!" Connie deflated him. "Let's go tell my Lady Luck we're one step closer to her secret."

They leaned on Lady's door and looked her over from nose to tail. With memory sharpened by the recent retracing of steps, Connie chortled happily at the contrast to the sorry thing Lady had been only a few months before. Now, where hollows had been were curves; where sores had been were no blemishes; and her coat, which had been dull and lifeless gleamed with the luster of well-polished wood. Her tail looked less like a discarded broom, and her mane of vital, live hairs was already long enough to fall over in a short bang.

"She'll never again look as she must have when she left her happy home; but if we can just prove she's got the breeding behind her, that'll be enough. Not that Silver and Midnight aren't good too, but I don't have any papers for them. With a registered mother and Golden Sovereign for a sire, goodness knows what a colt might bring," the girl mused.

"That makes me think, Connie. Since I'll be away at school so much of next year, I might as well be waiting for Waltz Dream to have a foal too—just to be in style with all the other mares. And I can't think of any horse I'd rather have for the sire than Golden Sovereign if it's all right with you."

"Pete, you must be clairvoyant. I've been wishing you'd say that. The more foals there are, the better check it'll be on him as a sire; and if we enter the horses in the Fair, we'll make a bigger splash."

"Hypnotizing me, that's what you've been doing," he accused. "And what do you mean *if* you enter the horses? I've never known anyone whose 'ifs' turned into 'whens' with such regularity!"

CHAPTER TEN

THE MORGUE

DISPIRITEDLY, Connie and Pete walked back to his car and got in, but lacking a destination they just sat there staring at Elm Street, Powell, Michigan.

"Lady Luck, huh? I think Mrs. Black Cat'd be a better name for that mare. Trouble, nothing but trouble, since we started trying to unravel her knotty past," Pete grumbled. "Well, what's the next step?"

"Moved out of town. No idea where," Connie mused. "They must have had some friends in town, if we could just find them." She thoughtfully gnawed on a fingernail, until Pete slapped her finger.

"How're you going to be glamorous if you chew your nails?"

"It wouldn't have been quite so bad if the people in the house now had taken it from the Millers—but no, there have to be two or three other families in between! Neighbors might remember though!"

Pete's door flew open, and he strode determinedly up the walk to the next house. Connie watched the proceedings, like a movie without sound: the door opened, a woman stepped out, Pete's lips moved, she listened, shook her head, motioned with her hands, her lips moved, Pete's head nodded, the woman stepped back in and shut the door, Pete walked back to the car.

"The Millers were very high-hat neighbors and had very little to do with them," Pete reported. "They moved four years ago about now (the lady was canning berries). They didn't live in Powell very long; daughter Josephine found it dull. The lady hasn't any idea who their friends were locally. Most of them seemed to come from out of town. So-o-o?"

Silence engulfed them again, and their two minds chewed thoughtfully at the subject.

"We could advertise in the paper, but it'd take longer, Pete." Without much hope, Connie watched to see whether he thought anything of the idea.

"The paper: that's the ticket, Con! If they were so swish, their going must have been chronicled in the local press. Let us hie us thither and search the morgue."

"The morgue!" Connie cried in alarm.

"The back files of the paper, little one. You don't find any corpses in this kind of a morgue. Only skeletons."

Finding the local daily was not hard—a tiny office on a side street. The only person in evidence was an elderly woman, who, though somewhat bewildered by their request, said it would be possible to consult the back files of the paper if they didn't mind a little discomfort. They renounced all thoughts of personal ease then and forever, if she would show them the files.

"Will you step this way?" she beckoned primly, and they followed. She led them between filing cabinets, stacks of indeterminate material and old desks, to the back of the shop and up a narrow stair into the loft. She stooped and peered and prodded among the piles of junk that littered the floor and sides of the room, interspered with large bound volumes covered with dust as thick as the tomes themselves.

"There they are. There some place." Her yellow pencil stabbed vaguely toward the most cluttered corner of all before she turned and with great decorum descended the stairs.

Connie stifled a giggle at Pete's ludicrous look of bewilderment. She tapped him on the shoulder.

"It's your move, Sherlock. You excavate, and I'll try and shovel off a place to put the book on *when* you locate it."

Clouds of dust arose at every motion in the room, and Pete's energetic assault on the clutter created a miniature dust bowl. Connie too was kicking up quite a cloud as she sought to improvise a table on which they could open up the bound volumes and search them.

"Ka-choo," bellowed Pete from his corner.

"Ka-choo," echoed Connie. "And to think that there are people who consider farming dirty work!"

"Thid oughd do be id," Pete mumbled thickly, dropping his selection on the piled cartons Connie indicated.

"Had we better take a quick look first at the society section and then, if we don't find what we're after, comb the whole paper? Or be thorough and go right throu~h?" she queried.

"Let's go from A to Z to begin with. You take the left page and I'll take the right," was his decision.

Pages flipped busily as their eyes scanned the columns in search of the name Miller. At first they saw only the columns of print whiz under their eyes, but gradually they slowed down enough to note some of the items. One or the other periodically read small items aloud, and it was so entertaining they almost lost sight of their original intent.

To discover that they had reached the end of the suspected volume surprised and chagrined them, and for a moment they were nonplused, but Pete proved to be a man of action.

"Well, I guess it's up to me to find the next number. Maybe Mrs. Whatsis has ever-bearing berries and lost track of what month it was."

"Good stuff," Connie applauded. "If you should happen to find the one before this one, pull it out too. Then we can work both ways from the center."

Pete ransacked the clutter, and after a few false moves he literally stumbled across both volumes at once. Again pages rustled busily as they scanned the columns of print, but their optimism was somewhat muted when the succeeding volume was completed with no success.

"Three's my lucky number," Connie stated defiantly, and opened the next tome with a thump.

Several pages had been turned, and Pete had his finger on the corner waiting to leaf another, but Connie lingered.

"Um-m, they moved after this date. Here it says, 'Miss Josephine Miller, daughter of A. N. Miller, 23 Elm Street, has come back to Powell from Beechwood School, where she was graduated with honors, including a scholarship to Abigail Aiton College for Women. Our congratulations to Miss Miller and best wishes for her continued scholastic success.' At least I'm glad to know that they really did live in town."

"Connie, wouldn't that be a lead? Why not write to her instead of her father, in care of the college? Her home address ought to be on file there."

"If we don't find anything else—the address they

moved to would be safer. After all, by this time she could have been in seven other colleges. Let's keep going until we're sure there's nothing in the paper."

At last Connie was convinced that the Millers' departure had not been noted in the local press, and they had to be content with making a note of the daughter's scholastic ventures.

"Phewie, let's get some breeze in our faces," Pete exclaimed as they emerged from the dinginess of the loft. "After an ice-cream soda, that is," he amended.

In record time they had returned to the farm and harnessed Golden Sovereign. Connie purposely left the gate into the field open, and so interested was Pete in hitching up that he didn't notice. Golden Sovereign was learning his manners so well it was hardly necessary for Pete to hold his head for Connie to climb into the cart. Pete joined her, and at her word of command Golden Sovereign leaned into the harness with such a will Pete's added weight went unnoticed.

Horse and cart flashed around the field in one direction, then in the other. Golden Sovereign, at Connie's request, showed off all he had learned, and then Connie headed him for the open gate. At Pete's look of surprise, she explained, "While you were away, we graduated up a notch to the open highway—if it's good and open."

Golden Sovereign trotted along like a veteran, and he carried his head so proudly the checkrein was often slack. They breezed back and forth on the old road several times, and Connie happily drank in Pete's praise of the horse.

"You'll think I save up all the hard jobs till you're around. Maybe you're right, but anyway since you are here this ought to be a good chance to do some real road work. He isn't really frightened of cars because he's seen ours enough, but I haven't driven him on the highway except just up to this cutoff and back. Here goes!"

Instead of wheeling at the end of the old road, Connie swung the stallion into the well-traveled highroad. His interest increased, for there was more to look at, but he went as steadily as an old horse. A few automobiles met or passed them, and just as Connie was praising him for his level head, they rounded a curve and far down the road saw a terrifying sight. A grain thresher hauled by a noisy tractor and followed by an accessory wagon was lumbering slowly down the road right at them.

Golden Sovereign stopped dead in his tracks at such a fearsome sight even that far off, and snorted with nervousness, but Connie was not willing to let him dictate their movements. She urged him forward a few feet to prove it was her will and not his that counted, then coolly wheeled the equipage around. He would have sped along, but her firm hands held him down to walk, lest he have the feeling of flight, and it was not until he had walked far enough to restore his equanimity that she touched him into a spanking trot.

Pete sat still until the cart was speeding away from the monster, before he exclaimed, "Wow! For a minute I was afraid you thought it'd be for the good of his soul to meet that business head on."

"'He who fights and runs away, lives to fight another day,'" Connie quoted with a grimace. "And there'll be another day without tempting providence. Anyway he's had some experience on the highway—enough for a start."

Golden Sovereign was rubbed down well, for his exertions and excitement, coupled with a warm midsummer afternoon, had lathered him. They took turns walking him about until he was cool enough to turn out. Free of restraint, his boyishness asserted itself, and he raced and kicked about his paddock. Every corner held imagined dangers, and he struck and kicked and raced around as though he had not just had a workout.

A lonesome bleat from Camellia's stall reminded Connie that one animal had been left behind.

"Poor girl, you'd like to have a little fun too, wouldn't you? But those nimble little deer's legs of yours would take you right over our fences, and you'd head back home." She paused and considered the goat. "Golden Sovereign's paddock has an extra-high fence now, and I don't see why you two wouldn't get along in the same place since you're such loving neighbors. Let's try it!"

Loosing the goat in the doorway, Connie and Pete watched with interest. Camellia expressed herself in a series of highland flings and side-winders, and satisfied that she was free, she trotted to meet Golden Sovereign, who met her with out-stretched nose. They held a brief conversation in mid-field before dropping their heads to graze. Camellia's teeth were not made for cropping grass, and she headed for the bushes growing along the fence. Docile as a dog, Golden Sovereign tagged along.

"Some horse of yours, taking orders from a goat," Pete jeered, but Connie was complacent.

"He's just being polite and making her feel at home. He's a true gentleman."

A few minutes later Connie sat at the living-room desk, thoughtfully chewing her pen. "If I'd realized how much letter writing there was going to be in horse raising, I'd have taken business English in school."

Pete lazily turned toward her from his super-relaxed position on the davenport. "Just let me know if you need the master mind. Helpful suggestions hinted and thoughts turned on and off while you wait."

"See how this sounds, then." Connie read her draft of a letter to Josephine Miller, erstwhile owner of Lady Luck.

"You sound awful snooty. Better soften it up a little, or she'll tell you to jump in the lake."

Connie returned to her labors and finally completed the letter to her and her critic's satisfaction. She pounded the stamp on with emphasis and handed the envelope to Pete.

"Don't forget to mail it before you get clear' home."

"Driving me away, that's what you are. And no confidence in me either." He shook his head piteously as he went out the door. "Just for that I'm not coming back until tomorrow!"

CHAPTER ELEVEN

BOOMERANG

TIME FLEW PAST CONNIE with the speed of light, notwithstanding her anxious waiting for a reply from Josephine Miller. Another cutting of hay was added to the barns, grain was cut and threshed, and granary bins overflowed with the winter's supply. Other signs of late summer were apparent: goldenrod and wild asters swayed gracefully through the sunny days, while at night crickets plaintively chirped their warning of approaching frost.

Golden Sovereign progressed with the season and, short of meeting a threshing machine face to face, Connie drove him around the country roads without a qualm. By a system she devised for suspending the cart shafts from the limb of a tree, she was able to hitch and unhitch him single-handed, and each day his heels clicked off several miles of training.

No perceptible improvement was visible from

day to day, but by contrasting one day's routine with that of several weeks previous, Connie gauged and was encouraged by his progress. His step was springy and stylish, his carriage as regal as any king who wore a jeweled crown, yet his disposition remained as sunny as his coat.

His daily drive did not end his schooling now, however, and after unhitching him from the cart Connie continued to fuss with him. Her grooming rags grew larger and larger, and frequently one was left spread across his back for quite a while. As time went on, the rags became so big they even resembled a blanket.

Her tiniest saddle happened one day to be hanging across the partition near their grooming stand, and Golden Sovereign's lively curiosity prompted him to examine it thoroughly with much snuffing and nosing. She sometimes held it over her arm as she moved around him, and though he rolled his eyes to keep track of it, he soon forgot it. Even when it brushed him he paid no attention until it was eased onto his back. He flinched at its first touch until he recognized it as only a larger back pad such as he wore when hitched up. The girth was drawn up so that he could feel its pressure, but in his easygoing way it didn't seem worth making trouble over.

This procedure continued for several days, and he soon paid no attention to the whole thing. He walked about the yard at the end of his lead rope, and if Connie threw her arm over the saddle he merely looked around in surprise. He had a similar reaction when a larger saddle replaced the small one.

Back to the beginning of his memory he was accustomed to seeing Connie climbing around his stall, either on the door or perched in his mother's manger, and it seemed very natural when she loomed up somewhere in his own stall. With a tight hold on the side of the stall, her other arm sometimes pressed down on his back or she leaned heavily against his side.

Returning from an unusually long drive one day, Connie left his bridle on and substituted short reins for the driving set. Golden Sovereign was rubbed and petted, even given an extra carrot or two, and the saddle was slipped across his back. His ears snapped back and forth attentively as she talked to him.

"Last night I wished on the first star, Sliver, that you'd behave today when I mount for the first time. I don't exactly want to hitch my wagon to a star, nor you either, but I hope the combination will bring us luck."

They proceeded to the field where their first lessons had taken place and, making certain that everything was sound and tight, Connie slipped her foot into the stirrup and swung up. Her hands on his shoulders broke the impact, and she settled into the saddle as lightly as a pillow. Caught flat-footed by this novel procedure, Golden Sovereign danced away a few steps, but discovering that she went with him, he turned to investigate.

Everything seemed to be the same, but instead of standing beside him, his friend was up above him. He shook his head, bewildered by this sudden change, but he recognized her touch on the reins. That felt familiar, and involuntarily he moved forward in response to a squeeze of her knees.

Horse and rider decorously walked around the field, circled, backed, and walked on. One thing he found different was the guiding, for when one rein directed him to turn, the other rein and knee emphasized it by steadily pressing him over, and Connie soon noted that knee and rein were answered before direct pressure on the rein.

"You're a honey of a horse—in every way, color, style, and manners," Connie complimented him with a caress as she slipped from the saddle.

Her work with the horses finished, Connie returned to the house by way of the mailbox. Each time she pulled the door down her hopes were high, but she had been disappointed so often the feeling of anticipation grew shorter and shorter. Her fingers tingled strangely today as she withdrew the mail and shuffled through it.

She squealed with surprise when one bore the return address of Josephine Miller, but she was reluctant to read the contents. If this were bad news, Pete and she would be stumped; but determined that it should not be so, she resolutely ripped open the envelope and faced it.

Dear Miss McGuire:

I was so glad to get your letter and to know that my Missy is in good hands at last, though I judge that she has not always had such luck. She was a darling and I objected to selling her, but a man my father happened to meet one day said she had a mean streak and was totally unreliable and might kill me. He said he had known her some place else and convinced Dad we should sell her. I did all I could to prevent it, but later when I went downtown they put her in this man's trailer and he took her away. I've never known where.

No doubt you had given up ever hearing from me, but the college forwarded your letter to our old address before it followed us to California, and then had to wait for me to return from vacation. After that I had to write back to the man Dad had commissioned to find a suitable horse for me—and all of this took time. He says that he got Missy from a farmer, sort of an amateur horse trader on the outskirts of Fort Wayne, Indiana. He can't remember the man's name, but says you can't miss it, because it had a white house with blue roof, red barn, green shed, and a big yellow hair-tonic sign on the barn. It's on the road to Lima, Ohio, and is about ten miles out of Fort Wayne. He happened to be going by and saw her in the stable yard and bought her right then. I'm sorry this is so vague, but it sounds different enough that it might help. If you need any other information I can give you, be sure and write me, and please give Missy a pat for me. When she left, I lost my interest in horses and have hardly ridden at all since.

"Indiana! It might as well be California for all the good it'll do me. And it's impossible to address a letter to a white house with a blue roof, etc., etc. But maybe Pete'll think of a way."

He was just as baffled when she showed him the letter, although he jokingly extemporized, "Dear White House with Blue Roof, I am very interested in horses, and as I understand you have a sign on your barn advertising hair tonic—"

"Have you noticed, Pete, no matter how far away she goes, she always comes back to this section, just like a boomerang? That must be a good omen. Your dad doesn't have any business in Indiana soon, does he?"

"No, worse luck. He was in South Bend just a few weeks ago, if we'd only known then. And I'm sure my jalopy would never hold out that far. I'll tell you." He brightened with inspiration and Connie's hopes leaped up. "Why don't you hitch up Golden Sovereign and take a little tour?"

Her disgusted look answered him eloquently. "Come on and look at the horses if you can't talk sense."

They strolled to the stable and talked to the mares, but Golden Sovereign was so deep in a confidential talk with Camellia at the far side of the paddock they left the two friends alone. Pete noticed the saddle hanging near the stallion's stall and negligently asked,

"When're you going to begin riding him? It's long past the time a lot of people begin breaking a horse to ride, and he's big as an ox. A flyweight like you couldn't hurt him."

"I've already begun. I rode him the first time the day the letter came—maybe I should have started sooner, if that's what brought me luck." She described how uneventful it had been and continued, a worried frown between her eyes, "He's so good, it kind of upsets me. Any colt is entitled to a little acting up, but he's just like a big dog."

"If that's all you have to worry about, I'll hide around the corner of the barn with a BB gun. That ought to stir him up enough to suit you."

Their friendly wrangling was interrupted by a car driving into the yard, and Connie went to meet the couple who stood looking about them appraisingly. She expected to be asked for a dozen eggs or a quart of milk.

"Good afternoon. Is this Shamrock Stables?" Too surprised at hearing the name used as a real place instead of in her dream, Connie could only nod.

"Dr. Casey sent us. We're looking for a place to board our horses this winter, my wife's and mine. We'll be away most of the time, but once in a while when we are around we'd like to be able to ride, so we want them where they'll get a little extra exercise."

Connie became very businesslike and, naming her rates, said, "If you'll come this way, I'll show you the stables."

She picked up some hay from the chute for a

sample, outlined the feeding plan, showed them the paddock, and added that if the owner wished she would be willing to give a little schooling to keep them in trim. The condition of her own horses was her greatest advertisement, and before the others drove away the bargain had been sealed and a day named for the horses' arrival.

Connie was briefly elated at this new step, but subconsciously she constantly strove to find a way to reach Fort Wayne. Her father and mother interpreted her preoccupation as being connected with Golden Sovereign and his education, so it was with some hesitation that Mrs. McGuire said to Connie at supper, "I know you're terribly busy with your horses, but today I had a letter from my cousin Emmy. She's pretty lonesome since her husband died, and she wondered if I could come for a visit. Your father can't leave the farm now, but if you'd be willing to drive me, we can take the car. I'd be afraid to start out by myself on such a long trip."

On the verge of suggesting that her father go and leave her to look after the farm, Connie waited for her mother to finish.

"We could be back in a few days, but I haven't seen Emmy since we were girls, though we've written each other regularly. It isn't awfully far to Lima, but I'd hate to drive it alone."

"Lima? Ohio? Sure, I'd be glad to drive you, Mom. When'll we start? Tomorrow?"

Openmouthed at her daughter's unpredictable reaction, Mrs. McGuire thought the second day following would be better, and for thirty-six hours Connie was in a flurry of impatience. One detail helped her to pass the interminable interval.

For some time she had been turning the problem of Golden Sovereign's first shoeing over in her mind. He had always gone barefoot, and as long as he trod on only the soft earth around the farm it was an unnecessary expense, especially since hoofs of flint were part of his Arabian heritage; but as his horizons enlarged, the need for additional protection was evident.

Dr. Casey had long since issued an invitation to bring the stallion over to the Laughing Horse for a visit of an itinerant blacksmith, but the latter was so irregular Connie had always missed his visits. This seemed like the ideal time for Golden Sovereign to learn about shoes, and while her mother hurried around packing their things and cooking food to leave for Mr. McGuire, Connie phoned her friend and arranged to leave the horse at the stables until the smithy arrived. She hitched up and bowled merrily along to the Laughing Horse.

"I'm ever so grateful to you, Doc, 'cause he's a little too green yet for a trip to town, but he really needs shoeing now that he gets out on the highways so much oftener."

"Glad to be able to help you, Connemara. Any special instructions for his care while you're gone? I'm not sure just which day that smith will come, or I could take him back to the farm for you."

"It doesn't matter. It's time he learned more about the world outside anyway, Doc, and I feel easier about having you and a man you trust handle his first fitting. No, I don't have any special instructions. He's gentle in the stall, and ordinary care will do. Feed him what you do the others —he eats like a horse," Connie grinned deprecatingly at her unconscious pun, "and I'm sure he'll get along fine."

Already her inner gaze was fixed miles away at the "rainbow farm," and the girl knew she need have no worries about her treasure as long as he was under Dr. Casey's care.

"G'by, I'll be seeing you in a few days," she waved in farewell.

The day following their arrival at Cousin Emmy's, Connie excused herself and, leaving the two older women to talk over old times, headed out the turnpike toward Fort Wayne. The countryside held no charm for Connemara, whose whole attention centered on the colors of barns and painted signs.

The miles unrolled rapidly, and it was not until she had nearly passed that the rainbow hues of the sought-for farm registered on her. No painted sign, though. She wheeled the car around, and as she turned in from the opposite direction the sign on the Fort Wayne end of the barn smote her in the eye. Buildings, large and small, sprawled all over the place; and since none of them was in very good repair, she was prepared for the unkempt appearance of the man who came out to meet her.

"Hello! I understand you sometimes have horses for sale." She smiled her most winning Irish smile.

"Yes—sometimes," he agreed shortly. "What sort of a horse are you looking for?"

"I'm not really looking for one now—that is, I mean I don't want to buy one now. But several years ago you owned a horse and sold her to a man who happened to be passing here, and I'm trying to discover where she came from."

"Don't remember the horse. Why're you trying to trace her? Was she stolen from you?"

"Oh no, I own her now, but I'm sure she used to be a fine mare, and I'd like to know for my own sake. I raise horses," she admitted modestly, "and having her for a brood mare would be wonderful, if I could prove her background.

"Try and remember. The man who bought her was driving by and saw her and bought her. Here, here are some pictures of her. This first one's the way she looked when I bought her, and this one and that one show how she has improved."

The man examined the snapshots minutely and his brows puckered in thought.

"Anything else about her? She looks kinda familiar, but I've seen so many horses since then that just a plain horse doesn't stand out much."

Connie quickly enumerated such marks as

seemed noteworthy: the forehead star, the bracelet scar, two white feet, her various blemishes, but
at each he shook his head. In defense of Lady,
Connie said earnestly, "She isn't what you call
'just a plain horse.' She stretches beautifully,
and looks as proud and stylish as a National Horse
Show mare."

"That's it! Now I remember her. Chestnut mare
with star—sure I had her. Not many horses that
pass through here look so doggoned stylish.
You're sure you really mean she wasn't stolen
from you?"

"Course I am. What makes you think I'm lying?" Connie countered smartly.

"Because I always thought she was too good a
mare to be in the horse-trading circuit. But you
don't look very far into the past of a horse that
the gypsies want to sell you. She was too good
to pass up for the price they were asking."

"Gypsies," Connie echoed in a pinched, hopeless voice. "Where are they now?"

"Girl, I wouldn't try to say. All I know is they
appear every spring and camp in my grove for a
few days while I sell them some no-good horses
and they sell me back some other no-good horses.
But there are no questions asked, and where they
come from and where they go to I don't know."

CHAPTER TWELVE

STUMPED

THROUGHOUT CONNIE'S VISIT with Cousin Emmy and her trip back to the farm, her thoughts milled around one word—gypsies. Few enough of these nomads had clung together; and those clans that did exist were so scattered that, except for stops along their north and south routes, which they followed like the birds in spring and fall, they were rarely seen.

Their road home lay past the lake and the Laughing Horse Stables, and Connie, for all her perturbation about Lady's past, was eager to take Golden Sovereign home. She dropped off there while her mother drove on alone. Dr. Casey

124

greeted her warmly, but a puzzled expression slid across his face.

"Did you say that Golden Sovereign is gentle in the stall, Connemara?"

"Sure, gentle as a kitten. Like a kitten he sometimes feels playful without realizing just how big he is, but that's all. Why?"

"Seemed to me he acted kind of queer once or twice. Nothing you could really put your finger on, or bawl him out for, but once I thought he was going to crowd me. Another time I honestly think he tried to kick me, and it didn't seem like an accident. If it'd been after his shoeing, I'd have laid it to frazzled nerves, but it wasn't."

Connie tipped her head to one side to think, but no such instances came to mind.

"Maybe it was because everything was so totally strange to him. It's his first time away from his own stall. How'd he act when he was being shod?" This historical step interested her most, and she lightly dismissed Dr. Casey's fancies.

"Pretty well, all things considered. At first he thought it was pretty terrible, but he's a mighty smart horse and quickly caught on that it didn't really hurt."

They talked while they were assembling Golden Sovereign's harness and were soon ready to hitch up. Connie took the bridle and slid under the bar into his stall.

"Hi, mannie. Glad to see me again?" she greeted him and reached for his head.

"Ee-e-e-uh," he replied, and in one maneuver

put his head in the opposite corner, and Connie suddenly felt uncomfortably aware of his threatening hindquarters. "Come here, you scalawag, and let me bridle you, or we'll never get home," she admonished, half in fun.

Doc entered the stall and the stallion submitted to being bridled and hitched to the cart.

"Keep your eye on him, Connemara. I still think he's busting to act up but doesn't quite know how."

She did as she was told, but other than giving her a whirlwind trip home, Golden Sovereign made no trouble. He fretted more than usual during the unhitching, but this was understandable, and it never occurred to Connie to mention the veterinary's comments to her father.

Her routine with the stallion was resumed, and though Dr. Casey's words buzzed annoyingly in her ears for a time, they were soon buried under other things, principally the conundrum of Lady's origin. Her thoughts went around and around like a horse on a longe line, without ever stopping but without arriving anywhere.

Absorbed as she was, Connie did not neglect any detail of the stallion's training. His white stockings flashed back and forth over many miles as he pulled the cart, and unhitched from that, the saddle was buckled on and they began all over again. Connie made sure that he got plenty of harness exercise in order that their horseback lesson might progress slowly and thoroughly.

A great deal of her attention was devoted to his

reining, with the result that his mouth stayed soft and responsive without any chafing or pulling. Truly as Pete had said, Golden Sovereign could have been driven with a length of sewing silk, and Connie bent every effort toward guarding this delicate touch. Their first few lessons under saddle proceeded at a walk, so that Golden Sovereign might grow accustomed to the added weight on his back. From that they went on to a slow trot, during which Connie sat, relaxed and supple, with a minimum of jarring to his back.

Their first canter was much more of a gallop around the ring, but Connie patiently eased him down to a proper canter, and as time went on his canters began with less and less of a mad dash. Weeks of practice adjusted their speed to a collected rocking-chair gait, which she sat as easily as a horse on a merry-go-round. Then there was the schooling necessary to break him into a canter on the right lead, at first by exaggerated turns and little by little minimizing them until he responded perfectly.

Before Connie realized it, Indian summer had come and the opening of colleges took away most of her friends from around Tyrone. Pete drove out for a final holiday before starting his new year at State. They rode slowly through the woods, gathering some bittersweet berries to adorn his room, as a reminder of the farm, and together they mentally gnawed at the knot which would undo Lady's past. To no avail, for such gypsy bands as might have been around had long since drifted southward looking for a warmer winter than Michigan offered.

"Already I can stare at a page of printing and pick out the combination of letters that spell 'gypsy,'" Connie laughed. "From now on I'll be a pushover for gypsy tearooms and gypsy fortunetellers, but little good it'll probably do me. For goodness' sake, keep your eyes open for any of the Romany folk (see, I'm even used to the poetic names too!), Pete. You'll be covering a lot more territory than I will, and that makes your odds better than mine."

"I will, Connie," he promised. "You know, I wish you were going to college too this fall. We've planned it for so long, it doesn't seem right for you to be staying behind—even if it's what you want."

"I'm sorry too, Pete. Now that the time is here I wish I could be going with you, but next year isn't so far off, and then I will for sure. In a way, I'll be going to college with you now. Every time you see a postman you can think, 'There's Connie going to her classes.'"

"What do you mean? You'll be writing to me, I hope, but that isn't going to classes."

"I've enrolled for a couple of extension courses, just to make sure my brain doesn't get too full of hayseeds this winter."

"That's the spirit, Connie. I should have known that you wouldn't be satisfied to pass college up entirely for a year."

The horses were stabled and cared for, and

still the friends were reluctant to leave. They stood by the grain bin at the head of the aisle and looked its length. From each half door emerged a neck and eager head as the horses took it to mean feeding time. Beyond the four mares who had the grace to combine affection with their greediness, were the boarders which had come in such numbers with the closing of lake stables that Connie had wished their barn was even larger.

"If you have to exercise all of those besides your own, you'll have to stand twice to cast a shadow by spring," Pete twitted her as he surveyed the horsy scene. "Don't scrimp on Golden Sovereign's time."

"Don't worry, I won't do that. But it's not as bad as it looks. The mares in foal won't need much more than just pasture exercise from now on, and some of the boarders aren't on an exercise basis. Just paddock freedom. I'll make out."

With her friends away, Connie concentrated all her attention on the horses, and notwithstanding her cheery assurance to Pete she was kept very busy. Her word was as good as a contract, and rather than slight the exercise of one of the boarders she would have skipped Golden Sovereign's workout; but since this was unthinkable, all her daylight hours and some of the darker ones were fully occupied.

Golden October days faded into dark November, and before Connie realized it Christmas was just around the corner. Many of her friends had returned for the holidays, whether from college or jobs, and though Connie had met some of them in town, they seemed in different worlds. Even the new fall of snow, which changed everything from an ordinary winter landscape to a Christmas-card one, failed to cheer her the day before Christmas as she drove home from her last-minute shopping.

The McGuires had dinner early, almost before the first star was out, but in spite of her mother's insistence that it was a party and that her husband and Connie dress up, Connie's feeling of depression persisted. Her father built a roaring fire in the grate, and they settled down with their books and newspapers.

Connie's mind soon wandered from the printed page, and she sat staring into the leaping fire like a fortuneteller stares into a crystal ball. Before she had traced herself and the stables to a ripe old age, her ears caught the music of sleigh bells through the winter night as a load of Christmas carolers approached.

She listened enviously to the sounds of jollity, glad that the horse-drawn sleigh was passing slowly, and not until the bells stopped in front of the house did she realize that they were coming there. Before she reached the door it was flung open, and Di and Denny and Pete and all her old friends poured into the room.

"Merry Christmas, Connie!" "Surprise, surprise, Con!" "Noel, Noel!" they sang in a babble of greetings, while Mrs. McGuire bustled to take their coats and Mr. McGuire went with their driver to stable the horses.

"Push your chin up, Con—you'll step on your jaw," Di laughed at her friend, who was still too dumfounded to do more than stammer. "But—but—"

"You're the toughest surprise I ever saw," one complained. "Every time I'd get your mother off in a quiet place downtown, who'd have to come along and butt in, but you! We were about ready to put a liberal supply of glue in the driver's seat to hold you there."

Mrs. McGuire miraculously produced some hot chocolate. While they were drinking it and warming cold toes by the fire, Pete ordered, "Run and change your clothes, Connie. We're going coasting soon as we guzzle this."

"What're you going to use to coast on—my one sled and the sleigh you came in?"

"Look out and you'll see. Now skip, or I'll have to get firm," Pete threatened.

She pressed her nose to the window, and by bright moonlight she could see behind the shadow of the big sleigh many little shadows cast by a fleet of sleds and bobsleds. Convinced, she raced to her room and was into her ski suit and back before the guests had finished warming up inside and out.

The night re-echoed to laughter and songs and shouts of derision when someone spilled along the Royal Bumps Route. A cry of alarm went up when a sled careened into a tree and its unlucky rider fell off in pieces, but Denny and Pete were snowballed for their hoax when the others discovered that the hapless rider had been a snowman.

Back in the house, mountains of food went down before the onslaught of so many robust appetites. There were constant skirmishes under the mistletoe, and the piano got such a working over as it hadn't had in months. The tunes drifted into carols, and the crowd, sprawled in chairs or stretched on the floor, sang of a night many, many years before.

Though Connie was reluctant to see them go, the group began to prepare for the trip home; and when the horses' sleigh bells could be heard coming from the stable, Pete disappeared momentarily. He came back in, lugging a large, heavy box, which he thumped down by the Christmas tree, and fixing his eye on Connie sternly, he warned, *"Not to be opened until Christmas."*

The sleighload had hardly turned out of the drive before Connie was down on her knees, poking and shaking the box.

"Ah, ah!" her mother reproved her. "Remember what Peter said. Better wait until morning."

"It's past midnight. I think I'll open just this one and leave the others till tomorrow. It doesn't seem appreciative to let it sit here so long unnoticed," Connie rationalized, and at an understanding smile, paper began to rip.

Guess as she might, she couldn't figure out what was in it, for it was too large to be anything decorative and too heavy to be stable equipment, short of a new saddle. The outer wrappings gone, she was still mystified, and inside the box were other smaller boxes. She opened one and sat down on the floor in surprise, a delighted exclamation paying tribute to Pete's choice.

Her dream became reality as she unpacked a complete set of stationery with the Shamrock Stables imprint flaunted at the top of letterheads, noteheads, billheads, envelopes—large and small —memo pads. Below the printed heading in dark green ink was the silhouette stamped in gold of a regal horse, head and tail high.

"That's really Golden Sovereign," Connie crooned. "That's just like the picture Pete took awhile ago—said he wanted it for Sliver's baby book. Isn't it too beautiful?"

Her dreams that night were not of reindeers and old gentlemen in red, but of golden horses and young gentlemen with red hair flying through the air and down chimneys. To Pete the next day, Connie grew lyrical in appreciation of her present, but he disclaimed all credit with a wave of the hand.

"After yours, it was nothing. Somebody else had to make it, but you made mine yourself, which counts more. It's a perfect fit, too. Will I swell around the fraternity house now in my hand-knit sweater. Say—" he accused suddenly, "I hope you didn't have to cut any of your classes to make it!"

With mock meekness Connie replied, "No, sir.

I could look the postman in the eye every day a lesson was due. And I got good marks on 'em too, what's more. It was the long winter evenings, sir, that made it possible, sir."

Talk soon veered to Lady Luck and their unsolved mystery, but neither of them had any new angles to suggest nor progress to report, in spite of several hopeless attempts.

"At last I'm stumped," Connie admitted. "I've no idea where to turn next."

"Don't give up, Connie. Remember she isn't Lady Luck for nothing, and we'll get a break before long, or I'll go back and camp in that Indiana orchard till the gypsies come back!"

CHAPTER THIRTEEN

TROUBLE

CHRISTMAS HOLIDAYS seemed shorter than usual to Connie since she didn't have to go back to school, but Pete had to leave before New Year's in order to make up an "incomplete" he had against him. Her horses claimed her attention again to the exclusion of everything else. Winter weather made Golden Sovereign's workouts on the cart impractical, and he was worked alternate days in the bitting harness and under saddle.

His tremendous vitality required more and more work, and it was Connie's pleasure to go for long gallops as long as the footing was good. Golden Sovereign was not a tall horse, standing only 15.1, but his stride was exceptionally long and his ground-eating lope took them miles from home. Seemingly he was tireless, for it was always Connie who reined in, while he would have kept going forever like a mechanical horse.

This strenuous schedule put him into such top-notch condition that Connie could hardly keep her eyes away from his perfection, which now was that of a mature horse. Muscles rippled under his skin like molten gold when he moved, and though he had never been thin he had filled out through the neck and chest and rump. Every ounce of him radiated vitality. His delicate ears moved alertly at each noise. His eyes had the sagacity of all horsedom in them, and no matter how much exercise he had he stepped lightly about his stall.

The mares in foal relaxed into the slower winter tempo and spent the time peacefully in their stalls, snug against the sharp air outside. Connie, at first with some misgivings, began riding Golden Sovereign into town when going to mail her lessons, or letters to Pete, but at his evident enjoyment of the trip she was quick to volunteer should Mrs. McGuire need some small purchases.

Uneventful though her first trip had been as far as the stallion was concerned, she created quite a stir among local horsemen who had not seen him before or had known him only as an awkward colt. His color, his style, and his good manners constituted a living commendation of her abilities as a horse trainer, and whenever any of Tyrone's horsemen saw Connie in town they began dropping in at Di's old stable for closer examination of her golden horse.

Pete had been back at college only a few days when Connie's mail included a short, cryptic note from him. "Great news! See you Friday night."

"Now if that isn't like that redhead! Writing to

get me excited, but still not telling me what it is and making me wait until Friday. Friday—he must be cutting his afternoon classes to get here that early. It *must* be great news. Now what could it be?"

Half exasperated that he had roused her curiosity without satisfying it, yet excited in spite of herself, Connie spent the remaining days stabbing about in futile efforts to guess his surprise before he arrived. First, of course, was news about Lady Luck, but that she discarded because it was not the season for gypsies and, such a short time before, he had been just as nonplused as she. Could it be some collegiate triumph? We-e-ll, maybe, but it didn't seem likely as few sophomores got elected to anything big. He might have come into some money, but that would hardly get him all stirred up when his father was already so wealthy.

Connie's mental gymnastics were only slightly interrupted by the arrival of a letter to her father from Camellia's owners, asking that he arrange to have the goat freshen in the spring. Connie's first impulse on learning that the doe was to be absent from the farm for a time was to look for a short-term boarder, but she abandoned the idea principally because there were no applicants.

Her thoughts slipped back into the same groove and went around and around, always to stop at the same query. What could Pete's news be? Friday afternoon she looked at the clock fifty times, and had her father not driven away in the car with Camellia, Connie would have been tempted to start to meet Pete, but a rattling vibration in the air heralded his coming and cut short her wild conjectures.

"You'd have to be the son of an automobile genius to keep that car of yours running. It's been living on borrowed time for years," she greeted.

"Con, guess what I did New Year's Eve!" he cried, ignoring her belittling of his cherished car.

"Now if you've gotten me all agog just over some social whirl of yours, I'm going to chop a hole in the lake and push you through." His excitement was contagious, however, and she relented enough to ask, "What did you do?"

"First, three of us fellows decided to go stag to a local dance. It was kind of fun, but on the way home—quite late it was—we passed a place called The Gypsy's Den. You know, one of those places where the candles are all dripped down around the old bottles they're stuck in, dusty windows, and stuff like that."

Indeed Connie did know. During her brief trips to the city, hadn't she been to some gypsy tearooms that answered just that description? Wild excitement boiled up within her at the word "gypsy," and eyes shining with it, she nodded mutely.

"New Year's Eve, you know, every place that sells sandwiches tries to get some sort of music and entertainment, and this place was the same. Not many people were left—just one or two couples at the rough tables—but the musicians, in gypsy costumes that looked as if they came from the dime store, were still twanging away.

"We ordered something, and then I began to notice the music. It wasn't really the ordinary kind of stuff—oh, things like 'Dark Eyes,' of course—but not the popular numbers that you hear all the time on the radio. They stopped for a rest, and I walked over and asked if I couldn't order them something. At first they looked pretty unfriendly, but finally one of the men grunted, and in no time they were teaching us the words of a little ditty we liked and rehearsing it together."

Remembering Pete's clear tenor voice, Connie could visualize the softening-up work he had done on them, but she didn't interrupt his narrative.

"Anyway, quite a little while later, I asked if they really were gypsies, and for a minute I thought I'd get a stiletto through my ribs. We talked on, and I discovered that they had stayed up north instead of going south with their band, but that they were all going to meet for August full moon. Seems that the gypsies are going to have a convention (or whatever they call it) in honor of the seventieth birthday of the queen of all the gypsies."

"Where?" was the only word Connie could form in her agitation, knowing that only the oceans bounded their domain.

"Up on Lake Huron, at the tip of the Thumb."

"Pete, can I ever wait that long? It's seven months!"

"I guess you'll just have to. Better be thinking up a good story, because it won't be easy to barge into a gang like that, find the right band, and just press a button and get the dope you want!"

Throughout the weekend she and Pete held countless imaginary conversations with the queen of all the gypsies regarding previous acquaintance with a chestnut mare, and in each one they came out with flying colors. In each episode they won the information they sought, plus other bounties that varied from half of her realm to the choice of her treasure to her daughter's hand in marriage. To the latter, Connie tossed her head and said that if Pete'd be interested in some wandering gypsy he was welcome to her, whereupon his laughter rang out so merrily that even Mrs. McGuire listened and smiled with him for a moment.

Midwinter dullness descended on the farm after Pete's visit, and for the first time Connie noticed Camellia's empty stall. Not until then did she realize how fond she had grown of the graceful little animal and how she missed the eager head, begging for a goody or just an affectionate pat.

Connie's mornings were devoted to Golden Sovereign, her afternoons to the mares, who needed but little exercise now, and the boarders she had agreed to keep in condition. A blizzard further emphasized the monotony and isolation, and made work outside impossible. But a day or two of inactivity were all Connie could stand, and she improvised a small ring in the space between the haymows on the barn floor. As far as space was concerned, it was sufficient to give the horses enough work, walking or trotting around the rectangle, but the tempting spears of hay that stuck out proved a great distraction to her pupils.

Golden Sovereign proved to be the least tractable of all the horses, and at first Connie attributed it to the confined working space. Instead of circling obediently at her commands, from time to time he reared up and his front hoofs flashed out—not at her of course, but it seemed to Connie that it was more in temper than play. Never once did she permit him to have his way, but each time he appeared more willing to argue the point.

Luckily the weather cleared enough for her to hold their practice outside. Once or twice around the circle he was tractable, but then repeated his indoor performance, adding a bolt that dragged Connie several feet before she could brace herself enough to swing him around. She sent him off on the other track—frequently a way of overcoming a stubborn streak in a horse—but after he grew a little bored with it, he was worse than ever.

"Maybe you've gone a little stale, mannie. We'll put you in for today and see if you sleep off your bad temper," she soothed him, but was unusually cautious in her handling of the fretful stallion. "Just one good crack with that front hoof of yours and I'd be playing a harp. Be a little careful, won't you?"

Her duty done by the other horses that afternoon, Connie returned to Golden Sovereign's stall to see whether his disposition had sweetened up, but for the first time in his life she saw his ears laid back in real anger, and he shook his head fiercely.

"Sure and you're in a dark mood, boy. I hope you aren't bewitched."

Connie pondered this new difficulty quietly and decided that perhaps the monotony of the bitting harness and longeing ring was responsible for the stallion's crankiness. Accordingly she skipped that phase the next day and began to saddle him. Here again she could see trouble and took the precaution of cross-tying him in the aisle rather than risk her former casual saddling in the stall.

This was all that enabled her to manage him singlehanded, but once outside in the saddle her confidence returned. Golden Sovereign acted like a sulky little boy. At first he dawdled, but when her heels and knees pressed him on, he shot forward like a catapult. The road was clear of traffic and he ran unchecked for a way, but when she would have slowed him down he fought for his head. Her concern was not for her own safety, but for the horse, and she was loath to hurt his mouth, still baby-soft from gentle handling.

The combination of distance, voice, and pressure on the bit finally brought him down to a walk, and in the cold air he steamed like a hot towel.

Then she was afraid he might catch cold, so she had no choice but to urge him gently into a school trot. To begin with it wasn't slow, but by degrees she eased him down to a jouncy little gait, neither walk nor trot, and though it hurt her horseman's pride to tolerate it, she did.

Miles and miles they traveled that day in the hope that not enough exercise might be the reason for his tantrums. He walked back into the driveway more docilely than he came out, but his barn manners showed no improvement. Connie worried quietly over this sudden change, and even his physical perfection was no balm to her uneasy mind.

"'Andsome is as 'andsome does, my fine friend, and cow company is all you deserve." Connie banged the barn door for emphasis and left him to meditate on his sins in solitary confinement.

She was distressed enough by Golden Sovereign's case of the jimjams, but at supper her father completed her demoralization.

"How's Sliver behaving for you, Connemara? Seems to me he's been acting kind of funny, and tonight when I fed him it seemed as if he snapped at me."

The troubled girl stared at her plate, her thoughts in a whirl. Could she admit that her matchless Golden Sovereign was turning mean? But not to do so might lull her father into false security and allow the stallion to really injure him. Her eyes met her father's, and he had his answer before her low voice confirmed it.

"He's been acting pretty ornery. Today I had to cross-tie him before I could get a saddle on."

"That's bad. He'd better get over it and soon, for I don't care how beautiful a horse is, I won't tolerate a mean, treacherous animal on the farm. Life's too short to spend it wondering whether you're going to lose an arm or get kicked into the middle of next week."

Connie nodded mutely, agreeing with the wisdom of his stand, but at the same time knowing that without Golden Sovereign her plans for Shamrock Stables would look as empty as their fine new barn would be.

No horse would ever get the best of Connie with her consent, and though her father had to help her saddle Golden Sovereign for his daily exercise, work him she did. She never returned from the ride with any feeling of satisfaction that his learning or performance had improved one notch. Rather he seemed to be going backward and unlearning many of the things she had so painstakingly taught, but she doggedly persisted, in the hope that a miracle would reform the unruly stallion.

Camellia returned to the farm, and they were undecided whether or not to risk putting her back in her old place next to the troublemaker, lest she get hurt during one of his tempers. Finally, rather than do all the shifting necessary in the new barn to accommodate the goat, it was decided to try it out. She was brought in during

Connie's period with the other horses, and the girl kept one ear tuned toward the stud barn.

To her relief all was quiet, and then it was time for Golden Sovereign's turn. After she and her father had tussled with the stallion, he was saddled and they rode out onto the highway. She was filled with a do-or-die spirit and determined that, if necessary, she would ride him till moonrise to take the meanness out of him. It was sunset anyway before they returned, and it did seem that the edge had been taken off his temper.

"Probably just wishful thinking because I want him to get over it so bad," she thought as she hung the saddle on a peg. "Hello there, Camellia. I'd most forgotten you in my worry over old smarty pants. I hope you two get along all right tonight. If he starts a rumpus just scream, and we'll come arunning and put you in a safer place."

Connie neglected her extension courses and combed her books on horse training to discover, if she could, the touchstone that would turn Golden Sovereign back into the sunny-dispositioned horse he had been; but though she found suggestions for biting, or kicking, or balking, there was nothing for plain, over-all meanness. He did seem a little better at his next lesson and, taking her cue from their heavy-duty lesson the day before, she rode him until she was nearer exhaustion than he was.

Each day she felt encouraged by results, and in a surprisingly short time he seemed to have become the mannerly horse he had been before. In reasoning it out with her father, Connie explained, "I guess until I began riding him to the limit each time, we just hadn't reached the point where some unspent energy wasn't left every day, and it grew and grew until you might say it burst into flame, yes?"

"Sounds as sensible as any ideas I have. Unless one of your little people decided to have some fun with you and Golden Sovereign."

Connie never wholly trusted the stallion again, as she had during his younger days; and though he gave her no further cause for suspicion, she no longer treated him as if he were just a big puppy.

CHAPTER FOURTEEN

GOLDEN DAWN

DRUMMING HOOFBEATS marked the passing of winter as Connie used Golden Sovereign's great energy for her trips to town. She greeted each balmy day enthusiastically as herald of an early spring, and almost quick enough to suit her Irish impatience spring was there.

With its coming, Connie's hopes and plans soared. Before long the foals would be born, the second year's crops would be growing on the new land, and it would be but a few months more before she could begin planning for college. Pete spent much of his Easter vacation at the farm, and when Connie asked him for suggestions on improving Golden Sovereign he could only shake his head.

"For a three-gaited horse he looks perfect. Anything else would be gilding the gilded lily, but he'd better keep out of dark moods like you said he had this winter. For either a show horse or a sire of horses, good disposition is essential; and if he gets in the habit of having mean spells, it'll queer him faster than anything."

Connie could only nod assent, but it had been many weeks since the dark spell was on Golden Sovereign, and there was not the faintest indication of its return. She did her best to insure against it, and his daily workout was enough to condition a horse for the Grand National, yet he pranced back as gaily as he left.

It was late spring when Connie thought of another tool for probing Lady's past. For the thousandth time she had thought through their steps to date, and then, rereading Josephine Miller's letter, the jigsaw fell into place.

"Chalk Scar took Lady to the Western Michigan people, so he must have been the one she meant who persuaded her father that Lady was vicious. That's as crazy as it can be, but he said he had known her some place before. He did, I'll bet, but didn't want anybody else to recognize the mare, so he took her as far away as he could."

Connie thought aloud in her excitement, as her mind jumped from bit to bit of the puzzle. "He had something he wanted to cover up, and with Lady around too close he couldn't do it. So if we could find Chalk, we'd be hot on the trail of real news. He must be a horseman of some kind, and that means that wherever horses are he might be."

Thenceforth wherever she saw a sign of riding horses, she stopped in on some pretext or other, but she was never any wiser when she left than when she arrived. At the first opportunity she consulted Dr. Casey, in spite of his notoriously short memory. He scratched his head and searched his memory, but he was no help.

"I wouldn't say I'd never seen the man, Connemara, but I don't remember him. Now if it was a horse you were asking about, might be I'd recall it; but a person, no. I'll ask around though. Tell you what you do: this summer you and Pete cover the horse shows. There're lots of little ones and some big ones around here, and if that fellow knows horses he's sure to be at one of 'em!"

Connie turned this suggestion over in her mind. As long as they were going to these shows, why not enter Golden Sovereign for the experience and whatever honors might be forthcoming? Trucking him around was the difficulty, since several of the shows were too far to hack him to, and hiring a truck for one horse would make it too expensive.

At Pete's next visit, Connie briefed her conversation with Dr. Casey and added her own embellishments. "But what in the world can I do about hauling him there and back?"

"That's easy. If you had been properly demure

and given me a chance to say more than 'hello,'"
he jibed, "I'd have told you sooner that I'm planning to buy a two-horse trailer."

"Pete, you are, honest?" Connie breathed her
query soulfully, overcome at such a coincidence.
"Where're you going to get it, and when?"

"Well—er—I'm not sure just which one I'll get;
been looking at several. But I ought to have it within a week or two—certainly before the first show.
Now that I'm going to own two horses soon, I
ought to have a trailer so's I can take 'em where I
want to and right when I want to."

"This is wonderful. I can hardly wait for the first
show. Let me see: that ought to be the Marchland's
Show in late June. Jiminy, I'll never forget that one
when I rode Midnight Moon." Her eyes darkened
with the painful memory, but brightened at once.
"This time I'll show 'em what a good horse *really*
is!"

The weeks flew past, and one weekend when Pete
arrived he not only had a horse trailer, but it was
hitched behind a different car. He ostentatiously
dusted a fender and caressed the door, and Connie
wasn't able to decide whether to be excited over
the trailer or the car.

"The trailer's beautiful, Pete, but how come the
car? Is it a loan 'cause Asthma can't pull the extra
weight?"

"No, ma'am. It's mine, all mine—or will be if my
marks next month are up to Dad's expectations—
and I think they will be. He's decided I'm a big boy
now and entitled to a suitable equipage. I bought

the trailer with my own money. It's a beauty—and not *very* old."

Nothing would do but that Golden Sovereign must have a lesson in entering the trailer. The floor was strewn with straw; stout-looking planks were lined up beside the tail gate, and one of the farm horses was led in first as a decoy. Connie led Golden Sovereign up to the trailer slowly, to permit him to look it over carefully, and then she stopped and talked casually to Pete, who stood by the entrance.

As soon as the horse accepted the new thing as just a part of the place, she led him back and around it several times, returning on a line with the place he was to occupy. The minute his hoofs struck the incline and echoed hollowly, he stopped. A tight hold of his halter prevented him from retreating, and Connie petted and cajoled him to allay his fears. She gently urged him forward, and with misgivings, his eyes rolling cautiously and his hoofs stepping high and gingerly, he ascended the slight slope into the trailer.

A carrot for reward was fed him by hand and some hay waited in the manger, and until it was eaten the two horses stood side by side in the trailer. Before he had a chance to forget this preliminary, Golden Sovereign was put through the same routine, followed by starting the motor and letting it idle a few minutes. Then Pete eased the clutch into gear gently, and they were in motion. The stallion snorted and would have jumped, but his tough halter and rope held his head straight forward, and Ted's stalwart bulk beside him prevented any other skylarking around.

A short turn around the farmyard and half a mile on the highway sufficed for his first taste of locomotion other than his own, but it had been so painless that he soon became as at home in the trailer as in his own stall. Once or twice they loaded him in, drove up to the old road, where his hoofs had worn a track, and took him out for a short ride. Loading into the trailer there bothered him not a whit more than in his own yard, however, and Pete and Connie agreed that he was ready for a circuit of the horse shows when they arrived with summer.

The mares that had been turned into pasture for short exercise now stayed in their stalls, round of body, and so filled with their secret dreams that they seemed to doze perpetually. Stalls were kept deep with fresh straw, and in Connie's spare time she made up endless lists of names for the foals.

One morning Connie made the rounds of the mares as usual, but since her father had come to the barn earlier, hers was only a tour of inspection. She patted the milk-white nose, the chestnut, and the black one, and was about to say good morning to Waltz Dream when something different about Midnight made her eyes search the stall again.

"Dad!" she yelled. "Midnight's foaled already."

Before he could step around the corner, Connie was inside the stall and, soothing the nervous mother, she dropped to her knees. A bundle of yellow fluff, hardly distinguishable from the straw heaped around, lifted its head and looked at Connie with eyes still surprised at finding itself in such strange surroundings, and a hungry whimper quavered in the air.

Mr. McGuire had joined his daughter, and together they examined the little newcomer, finding only perfection from tiny hoofs the size of silver dollars to a dainty white nose that already searched for breakfast.

"Your little people are with you all right, Connemara. This is going to be a palomino. I don't wonder I didn't notice it in all this yellow straw."

"Isn't she the beautifulest foal you've ever seen —next to Sliver, of course. I think she's hungry though. Oughtn't we to help her up?"

Her father nodded and, joining hands under the foal, they lifted it up and supported it while Midnight turned her head to nuzzle this demanding upstart.

Connie laughed at Midnight's bemused expression. "If you didn't turn out to be a fraud, Midnight. Just a few years ago you were trying to make everybody believe you were such a big, bad girl, and look at you now! All your fire has softened to a glow."

While her hands gripped those of her father's to hold the foal up for breakfast, Mr. McGuire asked her, "What name have you picked out for this little lady? From the way you've been working you'll have to give her at least three, to use all the names you've dreamed up—or are you planning that the other mares will have quintuplets?"

"Why, Dad, there's only one name I could give this one. She's going to be a lovely little palomino, and her mammy is Midnight, and after midnight comes dawn. So what else could she be but Golden Dawn?"

She was more pleased with her father's admiring whistle than with any words he could have chosen. Golden Dawn was eased back into the straw, and Connie turned her attention to the mother. A warm mash was prepared and offered with a bucket of fresh water, the stall was cleaned and fresh straw added, and when Connie couldn't think of any more attentions to shower on the pair she just stood and looked.

Golden Dawn had gone to sleep after her satisfying meal, but it was a short nap, and she awoke stronger and with another notion for food. Tiny hoofs felt for a footing in the straw and her forequarters reared up, only to drop back to the straw. Again she tried, and this time she scrambled up and stood on her own four feet, her tiny tail twitching from the effort.

"One thing sure," Connie said to her father, who had had to pause for another look, "she has her full allotment of ribs. Look at 'em—they stick out like an old umbrella."

"Don't worry. Midnight will soon put some fat on them for you, and love it!"

CHAPTER FIFTEEN

TWICE BLESSED

BEFORE CONNIE WAS USED TO THE THRILL of seeing Golden Dawn in the stall with Midnight, Silver Birch's foal arrived. Motherhood was not new to Silver, and her little filly had been washed and fed when she was discovered. Connie came back from a long ride on Golden Sovereign and at the barn door met her mother, who beckoned her into the other barn. Realizing that another long-awaited event had occurred, Connie clapped her mount into his stall and hurried after Mrs. McGuire, who explained that she had heard Silver's neighs and had come down to look after her.

The foal was already eating again, legs spread apart to brace herself for the important business of the moment and her brush of a tail twitching with every bunt she gave her patient mother. Like lightning Connie's eyes flicked over her from head to tail, and could see no flaw in conformation or color.

"Another beauty and another palomino. Jiminy,

Mom, I'm so lucky it scares me. It looks as though Golden Sovereign is living up to all my hopes. Two palominos out of two. It hardly seems that the law of averages can let Lady's be palomino too, but it's just got to be. She's the best bred horse of the lot—at least *I* know she is—and hers'll undoubtedly sell for more than either Midnight's or Silver's."

"Better get out that long list and decide what you'll name this one, Connemara."

"I don't need to do that, Mom. All I had to be sure of was whether it was palomino. The rest is easy. Her mother's silver and her daddy's gold, which automatically makes her Golden Treasure, or Goldy for short."

Mr. McGuire had come in from the field, and together they waited on Silver and Goldy to make sure they had every comfort. For days Connie could tear herself away from the foals only long enough to eat and sleep and exercise their father. They watched Lady Luck anxiously, but her foaling date seemed no nearer than it had been for weeks. That she would foal sooner or later was certain, and Connie could only wait.

May rolled on toward its close and Connie had to wrench her attention from the farm's maternity ward in order to prepare for Golden Sovereign's introduction to society, as well as an attempt to locate Chalk and learn more about Lady's cloudy past.

To Connie's great delight she had learned earlier in the month that Dr. Casey was planning an informal horse show and gymkhana at his ring for the day after Memorial Day. Making her debut on Golden Sovereign in friendly surroundings looked much easier than going off among strange people for the first time, so Dawn and Goldy were left to their mothers' competent care.

Notwithstanding Pete's final examinations, which must be passed with high marks in order to retain his new car, he promised and was on hand to serve as assistant handler. They paid scant attention to Tyrone's observance of Memorial Day and hurried back to the farm for Golden Sovereign's final grooming.

First he was given a warm soap-and-water bath, followed by rinsing enough to sluice him down the drain too. His burnished coat was brushed and brushed so that he fairly radiated light, and the creamy mane and tail were combed to such fluffiness that he seemed all cloud and sunlight.

"No matter how deep the straw, I hate to put him back into his stall," Connie sighed regretfully. "If he gets dirty tonight I'll be mad. What he needs is a set of stout pajamas for his back legs. Maybe I'll make some later—I've considered doing it for Silver Birch. With these light-colored horses it's not the initial labor, it's the upkeep!"

They timed their arrival at the Laughing Horse Stables to skip some of the opening events, so Golden Sovereign wouldn't have to stand around too long and get restless and excited. Connie was one of the last to ride into the ring when ladies' mounts were called. Her heart thudded with excitement as they pranced into the ring and fell into line with the other horses.

She was intent on the business at hand, but her ears drank in the "Oh's" and "Ah's" as the spectators paid unconscious tribute to her mount. Golden Sovereign was so excited at seeing so many strange horses that all his schooling fell from him in a flash. He pranced when he should have walked, and when the judges wanted a canter he two-stepped sideways, but Connie was satisfied that it was all in the spirit of fun and just to show off before his new lady friends. She never gave up trying and was encouraged to find him more responsive to her commands toward the close of the class. She won no ribbon, but his good conduct and the admiring exclamations were reward enough.

"You aren't really a lady's mount anyway, Sliver. This was just for the ride."

Golden Sovereign was entered in two more classes in the afternoon, and so accustomed to the bustle of activity had he become that he settled down to business enough to win fourth place in the Three-gaited Class. From an artistic standpoint Connie wished that the ribbon were something more colorful than white, but to the stallion who fretted at the tickling ribbon as it fluttered in the breeze, she confided, "The color doesn't matter today. This is just a dress rehearsal for other shows of all kinds when there're going to be plenty of blue ribbons on your bridle, and even some purple grand championships."

Golden Sovereign was being rubbed down and stabled when Connie's exclamation and wild look startled Pete speechless. "Pete! I was so wrapped up with the horse today I forgot all about looking for Chalk. Oh, what a ninny I am. But then, Dr. Casey knew we were looking and would have told us."

"Chalk wasn't there, Con. I took time out to go all around the ring and even snooped back into the stalls and around the trailers, but no soap. You can relax, but see that it doesn't happen again, or Kendall and McGuire, Detectives Extraordinary, will dissolve their partnership."

Sooner than he wished, Pete had to go back for his final bout of that term, and Connie too was in the throes of final examinations for her extension work. She signed the last paper with a flourish and saddled Golden Sovereign for the trip to the post office. They jogged along the road, in no hurry to shorten the ride, and though he hinted strongly that a faster pace would meet with his approval, Connie ignored his rudeness.

Her business in town was quickly completed, and after readying Golden Sovereign for their return, Connie lingered at the Lynns' back door to talk with Aunt Lou.

"Guess I'd better get started home anyway," Connie said in farewell, as Aunt Lou turned to answer the phone.

She mounted, but checked her horse's impatience at a hail from the house.

"Connemara, it was your mother. She asked me

to tell you, in case you're interested, that Lady Luck has foaled. I hope everything's all right— they're phoning Dr. Casey."

"They are! I looked at her before I left and she was just standing there, staring into space. Jiminy crickets, good-by, I've got to go!"

Golden Sovereign sensed her eagerness and was all for galloping full tilt toward home, but Connie was not too impatient to limber him up for a few minutes. Shortly, however, she lifted him into his ground-eating canter and the fringes of Tyrone were soon left behind. On and on they cantered. Several times Connie considered pulling him down, but the great stallion showed no trace of tiring. His legs drove along like pistons and his deep breathing was regular and easy, so Connie let him run.

"You're not half Arabian for nothing, are you, mannie?" she crowed, slapping his shoulder delightedly. His hide began to glisten with sweat, but still he ran easily, mile after mile, and it was not until home was a short distance away that they checked. The minute the farm was in sight Connie strained her eyes, but of course was unable to see what she wanted. Golden Sovereign was blanketed and shut in his stall like a flash, and Connie charged into the next barn. Her mother looked up in astonishment. "What'd you do? Leave your horse and get a ride in a car with someone?"

"No, he's in his stall. How're Lady and the foal?" she asked, hurrying up to the stall.

"Count ten, Connemara. You've got a surprise coming!"

Connie stepped into the stall, blinked, and looked again. Her eyes widened in astonishment.

"Twins! Is it really twins?" Doubting herself she stepped over and touched first one golden bundle, then the other. "Why, it can't be. Horses only have twins once in I-don't-know-how-many thousand times."

The call for the veterinary flashed back to her mind, and she whirled toward her father.

"Are they all right? Is anything wrong with 'em? What'd you call Doc for? I didn't even dream of twins, but now they're here I couldn't bear to have anything happen to them."

"There, there, girl, take it easy. We only phoned him because it's so unusual. We thought we'd better play safe. They seem all right—and so does Lady, as far as I can see. It's a filly and a horse colt."

Dr. Casey's footsteps echoed outside, and now it was Connie's turn to enjoy his bewilderment. He shook his head quickly, as though to clear his vision; but once he believed what he saw, even Connie's superlatives paled in comparison. No time was lost, however, in checking mother and offspring, and the McGuires watched breathlessly until he nodded his head in satisfaction.

"Everything's fine—ought to be no trouble at all. Now, you young hunk of Irish luck, I suppose you'll be glib enough to have names already picked out for the two of them?"

The older people looked with amusement at Connie, feeling certain that for once she'd be at a loss. She grinned gleefully, and hesitated just long enough to fool them.

"It's easy, now that I know they're palomino and a filly and a colt. You see, I had to make up names for all different possibilities. A daughter of Lady Luck should be Golden Opportunity and a son of Golden Sovereign is a Golden Ruler. D'ya think they're all right?"

"Couldn't be better," Doc applauded. "Shakespeare asked 'What's in a name?' but whatever there is, you're getting the most out of it. Perhaps now you'll be good enough to tell me the secret of your success. Here I've been working with horses all my life, and in your first few years you've done better than I ever will."

"I guess it's just my McGuire luck," Connie half apologized. "Dad laughs at me when I say the 'little people' are on my side."

"You might credit some of it to Lady Luck, you know," her father prompted dryly. "After all, she is their mother."

Connie tore herself away long enough to unsaddle and groom the unsuspecting father of the wonder twins, and hurried back to Lady. The others were still standing around the stall door in an admiring circle, watching the foals who had just stood up for their first meal.

"Looks as though you've some busy days ahead, Connemara," Dr. Casey greeted her. "I doubt that Lady will be able to feed them as much as they should have, and you'll probably have to help out with bottle feeding."

An expression of sheer bliss flashed across Connie's face at the prospect of being able to feed her darlings with a bottle. Neither the added work nor the possibility of late and early bottles daunted her, and she listened eagerly to the veterinary's instructions. "That's little enough for a person to do who is twice blessed."

At supper that night her father addressed Connie solemnly, "I'm worried for you, Babe."

"Not about the colts?" she countered in alarm.

"No, but I hope you understand you're having a terrific run of luck. No stockman ever has clear sailing all the time, but your luck is running high now. Keep in mind, though, that some day the pendulum just has to swing back. It can't stay perfect always."

"I know, Dad; I'm enjoying it while it lasts, but I understand that sooner or later the bad breaks will come. There's no use worrying until they do though," she concluded gaily.

CHAPTER SIXTEEN

LIKE MOTHER, LIKE SON

NEWS TRAVELED FAST, and it was not long before the McGuires saw more cars turn in their driveway in a day than formerly did in a week. It seemed that everyone in Tyrone had business near the farm and just happened to stop in to see the twins. Had Connie had a press agent to advertise Shamrock Stables, no better publicity could ever have been dreamed up than the birth of twins.

In saying that they occurred only once in many thousand times, Connie had been conservative, so it was not surprising that newsmen and photographers from the city heard of the phenomenon and swarmed out. The fact that Connie had bought the mare at an auction just to save her from going to a junk peddler added color to the story. Pictures were taken of the twins, of their father, of Connie feeding them from a bottle; and even the snapshot of Lady, taken soon after she had been purchased, was bought.

The one thing Connie did not permit was a picture of Lady Luck as she looked at present. It was hard to explain, even to herself; yet in spite of the fact that it might have helped unravel the mare's tangled past, Connie was firm that nothing should show Lady in a condition that would permit recognition by her previous handlers.

"I'd rather do it in my own way," she explained to Pete. "I know there was something crooked in her story. We'd certainly never get that on the level, and even if somebody did claim she used to belong to them, how could we be sure they were honest?"

"Who am I to fly in the face of feminine intuition?" he shrugged. "You're batting one thousand so far, with no help from the second team."

Gradually the commotion died down, and Connie could start a job with some assurance of finishing it without being interrupted a dozen times. Luckily, too, for the first real horse-show appearance of Golden Sovereign was not far off. Even his schooling had suffered from the flurry created by the twins' arrival, and Connie knew that unless she wore the edge off his high spirits there was apt to be trouble. For once he came second and Connie's first priority went to her bottle duties.

Marchland's Horse Show in late June was the first important event in the horse-show season, and Connie and Pete hoped that they might find Chalk there. Golden Sovereign was readied as much as time permitted and taken to the show grounds the night before with the thought that, by staying overnight, he would become accustomed to the different surroundings. Connie and Pete returned to the farm for the night, but were back at the stables early in the morning.

"That horse of yours is plenty handsome, but I'd hate to have the care of him for very long," the stableman greeted Connie. "He's sure no angel."

"Why, what'd he do?" she asked uneasily.

"What didn't he do?" the man countered. "Course, maybe it's because things are strange, and he'll be all right with you people here."

"Probably that's it," she casually agreed, but her gaze sought Pete's anxiously while they silently weighed the risks involved in entering a mean stallion in the show. Marchland's had been the scene of one of Connie's tussles with the unreformed Midnight Moon and now, years later, she had been counting on Golden Sovereign to redeem her.

It was still early. Golden Sovereign was saddled, not without difficulty, and Connie cantered and trotted him around the exercise ring until there was just time to clean him up for the first class.

The stallion's golden hide was buffed until it glistened so brightly it reflected some of the sky's own blue.

"Cross your fingers, Pete," the girl whispered tensely as he held the horse's head for her to mount.

The stands were filled with horse lovers from miles around. Those who liked and those who rode horses had turned out, and Connie felt that she was mounted on the king of kings. Golden Sovereign pranced and showed off to his utmost, sensing the admiration directed at him, while his rider showed it only by her erect back, the perfection of leg and ankle position, and sensitive hands on the reins. As if dissatisfied with his reception, the stallion tossed his head and a shrill neigh demanded "Behold me!"

Everyone but Connie relished this expression of his regal pride, but to her it had an ominous note. Golden Sovereign had never been a noisy horse, and this seemed a poor time for him to begin. She found comfort, however, in the fact that the noise and movement around the show ring bothered him little, and she shifted her position fractionally to be ready for the judges' first command.

It was to trot, but Golden Sovereign was having such fun showing off she found it difficult to focus his attention on the work at hand. First he cantered. She pulled him to a walk and then tried again for a trot, but his front legs cavorted in neither a trot nor a canter. Again he was pulled down, and after an admonitory slap on his shoulder he condescended to trot, but not before the judges had noted the delay.

Hardly had they struck into a trot when they were told to reverse and canter. This time Golden Sovereign really played. At times both front feet were in the air in a playful antic which steadied into a canter, but on the wrong lead. Connie checked him, bent his neck clear around, and forced him to canter, but he hopped and skipped so lightly she could scarcely keep track of whether or not he was on the correct lead.

She was working hard and welcomed the command to walk, but he had no interest in anything so ordinary, and loafed along, practically dragging his toes. Her heels jabbed into his sides in exasperation, and he shot forward so suddenly he nearly ran down the horse ahead. An imp of perversity seemed to have taken possession of him, and to whatever was asked of him he had to add a few personal touches of his own.

Naturally they were left in the center, while the judges examined further the horses whose performance had earned them the privilege. Connie had wisely pulled up on the end of the line, and after a few moments of inactivity Golden Sovereign tired of it. First one leg, then the other struck out in impatient pawing. Connie stopped that only to have him begin whirling. Pulled out of it, he shot into reverse, until the eyes of the spectators were less on the mannerly horses circling the ring than the unruly beauty in the center.

Connie watched her chance, and as soon as the

gate was clear she turned her horse and left the ring ignominiously. Pete was there to meet her and, with the reins over the stirrup leathers, Golden Sovereign was put into his stall. Immediately he made such a racket they knew he couldn't be left alone.

"Looks as though we'll have to take turns watching our problem child," Connie said disgustedly. "Have you had a chance to look around for Chalk?"

"Yeah, I've covered the east side, but quit when I saw you leaving the ring. We'll never find him if we have to stay with this temperamental Tommy."

"Well, you go and finish the other side and I'll wrestle with His Nibs to keep him under control. But try and be back before they call Road Hacks, or I may never get on him."

Pete disappeared and Connie's whole attention was taken up with the stallion. He continued to make such a fuss that she entered the stall warily and tied him up. Several discerning horsemen had recognized Golden Sovereign from his picture as the sire of twin colts, and they drifted back to the stable for a closer look.

They stood at a respectful distance from the stallion, whose rolling eyes and flattened ears didn't invite friendliness, and looked him over from nose to heels. Connie did her best to sooth the restless animal, but with no luck.

"Kinda mean, ain't he?" one queried.

"Not usually. At home he's gentle as a kitten, but he does seem to have sort of spells," she admitted.

"He's young and green, and so much movement and other strange horses around upset him likely," another offered consolingly. "He'll outgrow it."

"Probably," Connie agreed aloud, but to herself she admitted a doubt. After all, but a month before he had accepted his very first show with nothing but coltish good spirits, and the first time he got mean he was right at home. In Connie's opinion that theory was full of holes, but she kept her misgivings to herself.

"I've never seen a more beautiful palomino. Color, conformation, markings, everything's perfect. Has he sired any other foals than the twins?"

"Two others. Both palomino." Connie tried to sound nonchalant at this one hundred per cent palomino showing.

The man whistled. "You've really got something there if he keeps that up. There's no palomino stallion any place around here that's that consistent. But he'd better get over these mean streaks. Horsemen'd rather have a sweet-tempered horse, whatever its color, than a showy, mean one."

"What about his mother? She got a good disposition?" a second man asked.

"Not a gentler horse in the county. She's just like a dog—" Connie hesitated, but felt a half-truth couldn't go for a whole one. "Of course when she was younger she was pretty wild. But not mean!"

Her questioner shook his head knowingly, jumping at conclusions far beyond the truth. "That's it.

Lots of times it comes out in the offspring. Better watch him."

"But she isn't—I mean she wasn't—" The girl tried to explain, only to find that she was talking to herself. "Now see what you've done, smarty. Given your mother a bad name on account of your own cussedness. I ought to warm your pants for you—not that it'd help one bit!"

Satisfied that Golden Sovereign couldn't do much damage the way he was tied up, Connie sat down outside his door and gave herself over to worrying. Snatches of child psychology she had read in magazines returned to her, and she began as far back back as his birth to see whether anything she had done might be responsible for his moods. She searched and sifted through her memory, but she had gotten no further than his actual breaking when Pete dashed back.

"Didn't you hear 'em call for Road Hacks, Con? We'd better hurry."

Golden Sovereign by that time was in a tantrum and didn't care who knew it. At the gate he showed his disdain for silly circling of the same old ring, and refused to enter. Had he seen the tight-lipped determination of his rider, he might have given in earlier, but instead there was a battle of wills. At last he entered the ring sulkily. Other entrants had watched the argument, and once inside, he and Connie were assured of plenty of room, for no rider would willingly have brought a horse near.

They were the last inside, and the judges asked for a slow trot as soon as the gate was shut, but

Golden Sovereign wanted to feel the wind through his mane and would have flashed forward. Connie's flexible hands, yielding as rubber yet firm as iron, cut his speed to their compromise trot, and with mockmanners they circled the ring until the judges sent them into a canter.

This was the class Connie had had the highest hopes for. Golden Sovereign's size and schooling made him a natural for it and, had he behaved half as well as during their solitary workouts in their own field, it would have been easy. Now, though she knew that he was contrary and peevish, she determined that they would at least go through the motions. The class was a large one and the judges subjected them to a grueling succession of walk, canter, trot, walk, canter on loose rein, slow trot, gallop. The stallion's reactions were slow or, as it seemed, he deliberately misunderstood her aid, but she kept at it patiently, much as she would have were they at home alone—all but the cantering and galloping on a loose rein. There her good judgment drew the line and they rode with the reins still taut.

While the ribbons were being presented to the winners, she and the other losers rode out the gate, and Pete met her with a suggestion.

"Let's leave, Connie. I've searched the place like a bloodhound and Chalk isn't here. With Golden Sovereign in such a fit you'll never win anything and you might get hurt if he should go berserk!"

"Don't worry about me, Pete. I can manage him.

You know the only consolation I get out of this whole mess is that his mouth is just as good as ever. No matter how spunky and mean he acts, his jaw never freezes on the bit. He doesn't pull or take it in his teeth, and so I don't think it'll hurt to keep on. There're only two more classes anyway, and whether he knows it or not, he's getting good experience."

She smiled placatingly at her friend, hopeful that he would agree with her. Pete hesitated a minute, and she could see his indecision, but anxiety for her safety finally went down before her wish to continue. He acquiesced, but for the remainder of the day he stayed right at her side, except when she and Golden Sovereign were in the ring.

Having given up all hopes of winning a ribbon, Connie finished the show as if it had been only a routine schooling and handled the horse with as much consideration and gentleness as circumstances permitted. Unfortunately he wasn't as considerate, and his behavior went from bad to worse. Before the close of their last class she acknowledged the futility of it.

Weary, disheartened, perplexed, she felt too tired to continue the fight. Golden Sovereign was unsaddled and blanketed for his trailer ride. To test her and Pete's patience further, the stallion decided he didn't want to be loaded, and more time was spent before he consented to walk in and be tied.

Connie mopped her brow and glanced apologetically at her friend. "I don't know what I'd do without you, Pete. I thought he was going to grow up to be such a lamb, and already he's a two-man job. Looks like you'll have to be a permanent part of Shamrock Stables, or it'll go to pieces almost before it starts."

"Do you really mean that, Connie?" he asked, quietly yet intently.

Before she could reply from a Shamrock Stables standpoint, instead of the way she knew Pete meant his question, a voice behind them broke in.

"Miss McGuire, do you mind my telling you that your horse doesn't half appreciate you? You gave him a superb ride today, and one that many an older rider might profit by. In spite of his uncertain temper, you handled him quietly and with firmness so that your way always won, though not soon enough to suit the judges. But it'll pay you in the long run."

Connie looked with astonishment at the stranger. She had noticed him briefly in some of her classes, and his well-turned-out riding clothes and the horses she had seen him on added up to one who knew what he was talking about.

"Mind?" she half-laughed her exclamation. "No, I should say not. I was just wondering whether as a horseman I wouldn't make a better chauffeur."

"Don't get discouraged. Horses have as much personality as people, but you haven't the benefit of language in reasoning with them, so you can't hold it against a horse if he doesn't always see things your way."

Praise was never better timed than were the stranger's few words. Now her perspective was restored, and she vowed that somehow she would discover and overcome whatever was causing the trouble.

CHAPTER SEVENTEEN

ANOTHER LADY

GOLDEN SOVEREIGN SULKED for a day or two, and then unaccountably his sunny disposition reappeared through his clouds of temper. Connie almost agreed with the man who had attributed it to the strange surroundings of the horse show, but in the back of her mind lurked the contradicting circumstances of his other spells. Sensible though the solution sounded, it didn't tally with his acceptance of the Laughing Horse Gymkhana nor his mental seizure while stabled in his own barn.

Pete's Waltz Dream was supposed to foal any day, and so in spite of Connie's worry only half her mind was on the stallion's perverseness. Each day she stopped at Dreamy's stall to remind her that the foal must be a palomino.

"Nothing else will be acceptable, Dreamy, for you're the one purebred mare we can point to with pride and certainty. That doesn't mean I'm any less fond of the others, but your past is an open book, and your baby won't have a lot of question marks in its pedigree. Remember now, the honor of Shamrock Stables is at stake!"

The caressing note in Connie's voice lulled the mare, who drowsed contentedly, unmindful of the responsibility being placed on her. But when her foal was born, it was as though she had heard and heeded what Connie said, for palomino it was.

"For once you won't have to worry about a name, I suppose, Connemara," her father remarked while they tended mother and foal. "Pete undoubtedly has a name all picked out for it himself."

"In a way he has. He told me he wanted me to name it. Don't you think that a lovely palomino daughter of Waltz Dream should be Golden Music?" She laughed at her own glibness, but the excitement of the moment spurred her on.

"I feel as though I must be dreaming all this, but I honestly think it's an omen, Dad. Fate is showing me now that even if bad luck comes sometimes, my luck is strong and good and sure, and to keep working and hoping."

"Did you need anything to show you that? After the way things have worked out for you for years? You *are* hard to convince."

"And speaking of luck, yours had better get working for you on a cash basis if you're going to college this fall. In spite of the extra crops, I haven't been able to put much money aside in your college fund, so it all depends on selling the foals. Oh, there's a little money, but not enough unless your little people send you some buyers."

"They will, Dad, but I'm not in any hurry. The older the foals are, the better they'll shape up and the higher prices we can get."

Connie drifted along the line of stalls to look at the young ones, and in spite of knowing from the first that they must be sold, her heart pinched at the thought of parting with any of them.

"Maybe we ought to keep one, Dad, to train and show for Shamrock Stables. That's the best way to advertise ourselves, you know."

At her persuasive tone her father disclaimed all responsibility with an elaborate shrug, but he smiled good-naturedly.

"All right, but we'll be horse poor—and the day may come when we'll have to barbecue one of them, since we can't be turned out to pasture."

After supper Mr. McGuire had news when he returned to the house. "Lady Luck isn't the only proud mother of twins."

Mother and daughter looked up in astonishment, knowing that all the foals had been born.

"Camellia of Sunlit Acres has just kidded and is now bleating with pride over her twin daughters. They are pretty cunning, even more than a baby lamb, I guess."

"Yes, but goats have twins a lot oftener than horses do." Connie wasn't going to have anyone belittle Lady's exceptional feat. "That's good though. Didn't her owner say she'd come and get her as soon as she kidded? Now we can use that stall for a better-paying boarder."

Mr. McGuire had not exaggerated when he said

that the kids were cunning, and Connie delighted in watching their antics. Never had she known babies of any kind to be so smart, and when they were but a few days old they were running and jumping. Heights were like magnets to them, and they climbed on every box or rock they could find as they followed her around like puppies.

Luckily Camellia's owner was as good as her word, and soon came for all three goats; for as they grew older and braver, Connie feared that they might get into Golden Sovereign's paddock and be hurt. Camellia he had accepted all right, but to have two impudent sprites skipping around his hoofs was borrowing trouble.

All Connie's energies were pointed toward the big Fourth of July Show, which was the largest and most important of any show before the one at the County Fair, which climaxed the entire outdoor season. Both from the standpoint of showing Golden Sovereign to advantage and locating Chalk, it was of prime importance.

Early and late Connie worked the stallion, in bitting harness, hitched to the cart, and under saddle, and one by one the intervening days before the Fourth slipped away. At first she had come in whistling after their training periods, but she grew quieter and a frown of perplexity replaced her happy look.

Just two days before the show, her father watched her replace saddle and bridle after a workout.

"The stallion's getting mean again, isn't he?" It

was less a question than a statement, and Connie only nodded in reply.

"Maybe you're wasting your time on him. Why not sell him and keep Lady's little horse colt? There's no use killing yourself, even if Golden Sovereign is such a beauty."

"Dad, I couldn't bear it. And how do we know Golden Ruler wouldn't get just as ornery? He's Golden Sovereign's own son. And to sell him and start over is admitting I can't do anything with him, but I'm sure it's because he's young and has so much energy. He'll quiet down as soon as he's a little older—just you wait and see!"

"All I'm afraid of is you'll be quieted down for keeps too. There's nothing meaner'n a mean stallion, and it's foolish to run a risk like that."

"Tomorrow I'm going to work the daylights out of him, Dad, and he'll be better. You see if he isn't."

Mr. McGuire was almost convinced by his daughter's intensity, but when he saw her walking toward the barn the following day he strolled over to help. Golden Sovereign seemed possessed of forty devils. First he struggled against being saddled, then he wouldn't accept the bit until a firm grip on his jaw forced it between his teeth. But his final breach of good manners queered him with Mr. McGuire for good.

The stallion was too restive to stand while Connie mounted, and so her father held him by the bit. Quick as a snake would strike, his ironshod hoof flashed forward, and only Mr. McGuire's off-center position saved him from real injury. His face flushed with anger at the horse, but punishment, if any, he left to the horse's trainer.

For the first time in their three years together, the training whip sang through the air and stung against the offending leg. Golden Sovereign leaped and snorted, but his diminutive rider hardly noticed.

"One more trick like that, smarty, and you'll think there's a hive of bees after you. Are you all right, Dad? He didn't hit you, did he?"

"No, luckily, but don't you get off that brute while you're away from here, Connemara. I hope you'll be safe enough up on him, but you stay there. This time I'm not asking you, I'm telling you!"

Connie nodded acceptance of her father's ultimatum before riding out on the road. Golden Sovereign's powerful shoulders surged over many a hill and dale that day, and farmers who traded at different towns saw girl and horse gallop past. Many times the horse sweated and dried, and his crest was lower than usual when they re-entered the farmyard late in the afternoon.

Even so his unsaddling and grooming were as difficult as the preliminaries had been, and Connie carried a heavy heart to bed with her. Her mind went in a circle, trying to decide what to do. First, she would take Golden Sovereign to the show anyway and hope for the best; but suppose he really went wild and hurt someone or himself? No, better to leave him home. Sleep itself didn't still her mind's tumult, and she dreamed fantastic visions of trouble or of the stallion at the peak of perfection.

Pete's car rolled into the yard just after sunup and backed into position before the trailer. He looked up in greeting as Connie's feet crunched on the gravel.

"Hey, what's this? Lying abed too late to be in your riding clothes? Tsk, tsk, you'll have to hurry!"

"Golden Sovereign's not going. He's turned awful mean again. I guess I was right when I thought my luck was too good to last. He's furnished the 'Boom!' that I said might come and smash all my fine plans into a million pieces."

"Don't ever think it, Connemara Anastasia McGuire. He'll snap out of it someday for keeps. Come on, I'll help you turn him into the paddock to meditate on his sins."

Full of gratitude at Pete's acceptance of the decision and his conviction that Golden Sovereign wouldn't stay mean always, Connie walked to the stable. Had Pete needed any illustration of the stallion's frame of mind, their reception would have been sufficient. Teeth flashed, and he screamed in anger as they appeared. Pete noted that for the first time the upper half of the door was shut and tightly latched.

"Wow! I see what you mean. He'd sure be a dandy little playmate at a horse show, wouldn't he?"

Pete took a long, slender pole, and by thrusting it through the upper slats of the stall, he unhooked the outside door latch.

Connie flung her parting shot: "Now, you old meanie, you can prowl back and forth as long as you like and we won't have to go in with you. And I hope you get good and lonesome." She gave back glare for glare at the furious horse, turned, and left with Pete.

En route to the show Connie detailed her most recent troubles with the stallion and climaxed them with her father's suggestion that they sell him, but Pete's encouragement helped, and before they had parked and mingled with the holiday crowds her thoughts were turning hopefully toward their search for Chalk.

Their hopes were temporarily dashed after a quick circuit of the ring and a scrutiny of the stands, but since it was still early she wasn't concerned. They found seats which gave them not only a good view of the ring but also of some of the behind-the-scenes activity.

Connie would not have been Connie if the sight and smell of spirited horses did not brush away her cobwebs of worry, and with the opening announcement she began to enjoy the day. Not that she forgot her own horses. Each entry she looked at was measured and judged and compared with her own; nor was she unfair in her decisions. If a horse appeared superior to one of hers, she acknowledged it; but nowhere did she see one that could outpoint Golden Sovereign in anything except disposition.

Lunchtime came and still no sign of a man with a chalk-white scar across his face, but it didn't affect their appetites. Connie and Pete stood in the crowd by the lunch stand, munching hot dogs and ice-cream cakes.

"Seems as though he'd be here by now if he were coming," Pete grumbled.

"Not necessarily. If he's a horseman, he might have had to work this morning, or maybe he likes to sleep late, or any one of a number of reasons could have kept him away," she parried.

They wandered around, looking at the picketed horses, talking to friends, and generally killing time until the afternoon classes should start.

"There's Jubilee, the mare you first wanted to get, Pete. Ever been sorry you bought Dreamy instead?" Connie nodded toward a spirited bay whose impatient hoofs had dug a hole which her front feet had to stand in.

"Nope. She's a beauty, but she doesn't have anything to balance her spirits. Now Dreamy has spirit plus good sense for ballast, and she's not so likely to get herself into trouble that way."

So interested had they become in their tour of the horses that they had to hurry back to their seats, as the first horses were already in the ring. Connie tripped in excitement and, grabbing Pete's arm, she whispered, "Look at the man on the black gelding!"

It was Pete's turn to nearly fall over himself in excitement. "He's it! He's it!"

Their search, or part of it, was over. Even at a distance the narrow white line from temple to chin was plain, and it was equally plain that he was a real horseman. His mount was perfection, and his handling of him equally perfect. Connie and Pete climbed to their places and watched the class with intense absorption. The gelding never put down a wrong foot, and they took it as a good omen that he won the blue ribbon.

The program stated that Todd Jessup was the rider of Demitasse, owned by Hidden Hill Stock Farm.

"Don't let's talk to him here, Pete, if Hidden Hill isn't too far away."

"Good idea, no matter how far Hidden Hill is. Must be close enough to truck horses here, so we ought to be able to manage it. He's too busy and excited now to have any idea about a horse he hasn't seen for years."

"Tomorrow we'll go, huh? I can hardly wait. Think of it, maybe we're right on the brink of finding out everything about Lady." Connie was hugging herself with excitement, and the rest of the afternoon they had eyes for only the horses ridden by Todd Jessup.

"Pete, look at that mare! I'll bet it's her sister."

The class was for combination horses shown in harness and under saddle, and truly it might have been Lady Luck several years younger. Her color and markings and manner of going were so identically Lady's that, but for the latter's scars and signs of hard usage, Connie would have sworn they were doubles. Unconsciously, Connie looked for the bracelet scar on her right hind leg.

"Look, the program says it's Shady Lady. Either

it's Lady's mother or daughter or full sister. I knew our Lady's name must have been Lady, the way she recognized it."

That made it harder than ever to refrain from rushing down and talking with the man immediately, but some sixth sense prevented. They were content to snoop about and discover the address and how to reach Hidden Hill. From a discreet distance they watched Todd Jessup load the horses into a fine new van.

"Must be quite an outfit," Pete deduced. "Those trucks with custom-made bodies don't grow on bushes. Not even on trees!"

CHAPTER EIGHTEEN

HALF OF NOTHING

PETE STAYED TO SUPPER, and then, at the Mc-
Guires' warm insistence, he stayed the night.
Connie was all for starting at dawn, but Pete succeeded in delaying her a few hours by arguing
that dragging the man out of bed wouldn't make
him any more talkative.

"Better to arrive about mid-morning, while he's
out with the horses—that way we can look around
better."

One look at Golden Sovereign, still in his tower-
ing rage, satisfied them that there was no use in
spending time with him, and so they whiled away
a few hours playing with the colts. On the way to
the barn Connie had pointed to the pasture and

paddocks, saying, "Preview of Shamrock Stables."

Spread before them in the summer sun was a scene to warm any horseman's heart. Mares and golden foals were scattered across the green grass. Beyond in his paddock Golden Sovereign strutted and neighed defiance to the world, and all around was the abundance of nature to provide for the horses and their comfort.

"Instinct is a powerful thing," Pete mused as they neared the pasture fence. "How many generations do you suppose it has been since those mares' maternal forebears had to protect their foals from wolves and other wild animals? Yet when her baby's sleeping, each one of them stands with her head and forequarters over it, leaving her powerful hind legs for defense from any part of the circle."

"You'd better be careful when you go near 'em then," Connie cautioned.

"Why, for the love of Mike?"

"Aren't you supposed to be a wolf?" she finished slyly.

Pete laughed heartily at the dig. "No, didn't you know? I'm really a sheep in wolves' clothing."

They walked toward the colts, which by now had lost their ribby look, though their legs still seemed to be the biggest part of them. They stared with wide eyes at the strange animals that walked on their hind legs and hastily ran behind their mothers for protection, but as even this refuge deliberately walked toward the intruders they could but follow.

"Looks like I've been spending so much time on their pappy I've forgotten his children need attention," Connie observed. "Isn't it 'most time to go now?"

"Guess we might as well, or I'll be pestered to pieces," Pete surrendered. "But I warn you, I'm not going to drive fast, and there's no need trying to hurry me!"

Connie was enchanted with Hidden Hill Stock Farm before the beautifully kept houses, barns, and stables came into view. On each side of the road stretched lush stands of hay and rolling tree-spotted pastures. Well-kept fences contained more fine horses than the girl had seen in one place except at a show.

The big house seemed open, but no one appeared, so Pete drove on to the stables. Todd Jessup in person poked a head through a screen door and waited for them to state their business.

"My name's Pete Kendall, Mr. Jessup, and my friend is Connie McGuire. Yesterday we admired your horses at the show so much we thought we'd drop in, if you don't mind, and see them at close range."

"Fine, sure, glad to have you kids. Wait a minute till I stamp this letter and I'll take you around."

He withdrew, and Pete took this chance to whisper to Connie, "I'm leaving all the stuff about the horse to you, just to make sure we don't get ourselves all jammed up with two or three different stories."

"Great place you have here, Mr. Jessup. Must have taken you some time to develop it."

"Oh, it's not mine," their host disclaimed, though obviously flattered that they had thought so. "I'm only the manager and trainer. Boss'll be back this week."

"How could he leave such a perfect place?" Connie wondered aloud. "But I suppose it's just a hobby with him."

"That's just what it is, miss. Fact he hardly spends one month out of the whole year here. Most of the time he's in the East, where his home is, but he phones me once a week and we talk over everything. He depends on my judgment, and generally what I say goes." His chest expanded an extra fraction of an inch when he made the statement.

They had entered the large, airy stable and Connie was genuinely interested in Jessup's discourse about each horse. So engrossed was she in the horse talk she blinked with surprise when they stopped before Shady Lady's box.

"Now there's a real horse," Pete exclaimed admiringly.

"Amen to that, Pete. Where'd she come from, the East too?" Connie turned to their guide for information.

"No, ma'am. That little lady was foaled right here at Hidden Hill. Both her sire and dam are still here; she's out of Lady Baltimore by Bad Actor."

"Got any others like her? I guess not. She looks

like a once-in-a-lifetime horse." Connie probed with false casualness.

"Here's one you'll recognize too. Hello, Demi, old fellow." Jessup had passed to the next stall, and neither of the young people was sure whether he had not heard Connie's question or whether he had deliberately ignored it.

They passed down the row of stalls, Jessup reciting pedigrees and bits of information about each occupant, and Connie drank it all in with such glistening eyes he rather fancied himself a spellbinder. Standing in the big door, he waved his hand toward the knolls.

"That's the brood mares' pasture." He waved the other hand toward another barn. "There's the stud barn. Want to go through that?" he offered, impelled by the shining admiration in Connie's face.

"Oh yes, if they aren't mean. There's nothing more terrifying than a mean stallion."

"Why, they're all gentle as kittens. No reason for a stallion to be mean if he gets enough exercise and proper care. Oh, of course, once in a while one goes sour, but there's generally a good reason if you can find it. And I do!"

Connie looked the three stallions over with a careful eye, but not one excelled Golden Sovereign, and two didn't even approach his perfection in her opinion. But there was no denying that their tempers were much sweeter than his. It was little comfort to know that just once in a while one might go sour, if the sour one was yours!

"What'd you say your boss' name is? Or is he

Mr. Hidden Hill?" she prompted as they walked toward the car.

"You're partly right. He is Mr. Hill, but M. O. Hill, not Hidden. And a good guy," he added.

"It'll be nice for you having him here for a while. Must be funny to work for a man you hardly ever see," Pete commented.

"Funny thing is, I won't be here. Got to take a vanload of horses down to Kentucky—that's one of the reasons he's coming out, to superintend things while I'm away."

Pete trod on the starter and the engine snorted to life. They were about to slip into gear when Connie reached into her purse and drew out the snapshot.

"Ever see that horse before, Mr. Jessup?"

He half concealed his start of surprise. He smiled sarcastically.

"Sure, just showed her to you—or haven't you much memory for horses?"

"Maybe better than yours seems to be. That isn't Shady Lady. Could she have had a sister?"

"I don't know what you're talking about. I've never seen the horse. Wait a minute though; let me see the picture closer."

"Oh, no! You're close enough to see it looks like Shady Lady. All you have to say is 'yes' or 'no.' Did she ever have a sister?"

"Get out. That's what I say, you bumptious brats." No longer was Todd Jessup the affable braggart. Connie's words had changed him into a thin-lipped man whose scar stood out red as fire on a chalk-white face.

The car jumped forward, and their last glimpse was of Jessup banging into the office.

"I guess I wasn't very diplomatic," Connie ruefully admitted.

Pete's laugh rang out above the motor noise. "You don't mean it. What makes you have any such suspicion as that?"

"It's the end of the trail, Pete. There's something funny all right, or he wouldn't have lied and said he'd never seen her when we knew he had at least once—unless the Western Michigan Livestock people dreamed him. He's trying to cover something up, but how're we going to prove it?"

"You've got me, Con. It won't be easy, and you can bet Jessup will balk us if he possibly can. *We* know where Lady came from, but unless we show it in black and white no one else'll believe us."

"The gypsies must be the only missing link, judging by the Lady's age (if that's polite) and how long they've had Lady Baltimore. We've just got to see those gypsies next month." Connie's jaws closed with determination.

"What if it rains during August full moon? S'pose the gypsies will still have their gathering of the clans?" Connie turned to Pete, her lips parted in alarm, but smiled sheepishly when she saw that he was joking.

The car hummed along for a time before Connie jumped to another topic: "You realize what today is, Pete?"

He cocked his head and considered. "It's the fifth of July. The day after the Fourth. Sure! It's Golden Sovereign's birthday!"

"He's a big boy of three now. And old enough to know better," Connie amended, her thoughts on his captious temper. "Maybe I should have kidded Mr. Jessup along a little, and he'd surely have been able to find out what makes Golden Sovereign go so sour. There's nothing Mr. Jessup thinks Mr. Jessup can't do!"

Later Connie leaned over the stall door and addressed the twins, "Hello, little spooks. That's what you must be, because your mammy never was nothing, not even a horse. So that means you're only half of nothing apiece."

She and Pete silently contemplated their sleuthing job.

"Well, Pete, what d'ya think we'd better do next?"

"Same thing you're thinking—wait until Jessup's gone to Kentucky, and go back and talk with the boss."

"It's not fair reading my mind like that. That'll be at least a week. And that'll seem more like a month. Wish it were tomorrow."

Mr. McGuire walked into the door and hailed them cheerily. "Well, young 'uns, I mowed the big field today, and haying starts tomorrow in earnest. Know of any men around for hire?"

" 'The devil finds work for idle hands to do,' " Pete quoted solemnly, his eyes turned skyward.

CHAPTER NINETEEN

MR. HILL OF HIDDEN HILL

HAYING OPERATIONS PROGRESSED day after day, and each nightfall Connie felt that much closer to meeting Mr. Hill. Surely they would get a hint which would enable them to prove Lady's existence. The work horses became accustomed to hearing Connie carrying on long imaginary conversations with the owner of Hidden Hill, and though they varied in introduction and content, the conclusion was always the same.

The only incident which marked the passing of days was Mrs. McGuire's greeting one evening when they came in from almost their last day in the fields: "I think we ought to change Camellia's name to Finnegan."

"Why, Mom? She isn't our worry any more, or is she?" Connie hesitated, and the words of the old rhyme repeated themselves, "Off again, on again, gone again, Finnegan."

"You mean she's back again—and the kids?"

"Yes, she's back again, but not the kids. They've

been sold. Her owner is sick, and her husband didn't want to be bothered with the milking. At first I wasn't going to take her, remembering what you said about a better-paying boarder, but they were willing to pay more because she's used to this place now."

"They did say that we'd have the milk extra, but I pointed out that we already had cows and they were welcome to it if they wanted to come out and milk her!" Mrs. McGuire tossed her head as she recounted her brush with Camellia's owners.

"Where is she? All the stalls are full."

"Oh, I just turned her into Golden Sovereign's paddock."

"Jiminy, Mom, that's pretty risky, and him in such a mean mood."

Her mother airily dismissed Connemara's concern. "They seemed to get along all right, and I haven't heard any fracas. You can put Camellia Finnegan any place you can find for her."

The evening chores finished, Connie gingerly lured Camellia out of Golden Sovereign's paddock with a pan of grain, but then didn't know where to put her. As a temporary measure, she was finally walled off in the alley outside his stall. His was the end one, and since he had been left to himself, the space outside was not needed.

Realizing that the morrow would finish haying and their week of waiting, Connie promptly forgot everything else but the impending talk with Mr. Hill, and at long last she and Pete were on their return trip to Hidden Hill. With their eyes, they reconnoitered as the car approached the gate and the way seemed clear. No sooner had they driven in, however, than a stable hand appeared from nowhere and ordered them to leave.

"We want to see Mr. Hill."

"He ain't here, and if he was you couldn't see him. Git out!"

Connie's darting eyes had spotted an expensive-looking car at the side of the house. "He is, too, and we want to see him." Deliberately her voice rose, shrill and penetrating.

Their opposition glared balefully. "If he is or if he ain't here, you get out and don't come back. We're onto your sneaky ways!"

Connie's mouth opened to argue further, but a man stepped out of the front door of the big house.

"What's going on here and why the uproar? Grimes, what is this?"

"These people were here last week, and when Mr. Jessup's back was turned they deliberately tried to harm one of the horses."

Such an unjust accusation left Connie and Pete unprepared for a defense, but not for long. Her eyes flashing, Connie snapped, "That's a barefaced lie, Mr. Hill. We were here last week, but harming one of your horses—or any horse—is the last thing we want to do. We really came back to talk to you about something we think it's to your own interest to hear."

He looked from one to the other, undecided as to whom to believe. Certainly they hurt no one standing in the middle of his driveway. He nodded.

"All right. Here I am. What's on your mind?"

Connie exhaled with relief. Digging frantically into her purse, she extracted Lady's picture and handed it to him.

"Did you ever own that horse, Mr. Hill? It's not Shady Lady," she cut off his obvious retort. "This picture was taken at my home, long before I knew Shady Lady existed."

"No, I have no horse that this could be." He returned the snapshot.

"Oh!" Her toneless monosyllable echoed her disappointment, and such dejection made him unbend a little.

"It's a curious thing. That does remind me somewhat of a mare I used to own—"

Connie's hopes flared like rockets, but his upheld hand silenced her.

"But she broke a leg and had to be destroyed. Her grave is up there under the oaks."

"That's what we meant, Mr. Hill. A mare you used to have but don't any more. I've got her now, I'm sure, and this is her picture."

"My dear young lady, I just explained that that horse is dead. Shot through the head, so you couldn't possibly own her—unless you go in for nightmares," he smiled condescendingly.

"Did you see her broken leg? Did you see her shot? Did you help to bury her?"

Connie's questions pelted him like hailstones, and annoyed him as much.

"Certainly not. I am not in the habit of shooting my horses. Grimes, you tell them about it."

"Well, as a matter of fact, Boss, I wasn't here either then. You see—Mr. Jessup called me at home one morning and gave me a day off. He said it'd be a good chance to get my tooth fixed. I remember his telling the next day what a time he had had with the team, making 'em haul the dead mare up the hill."

"See what I mean, Mr. Hill," Connie hinted. "I'll bet he had a time—but he couldn't wait till Mr. Grimes came back. Who else didn't see it?"

"Miss What-ever-your-name-is, if you're suggesting that Jessup is dishonest you can save your breath. He has been with me for years, and I'd trust him with anything I own."

"Shall I throw 'em out, Boss?" Grimes asked hopefully.

"Probably she wasn't a very valuable mare if you're not more concerned than this about her." No horseman can bear to have his animals belittled, and Connie heavily accented the derogatory remark.

"It just happens that she was about the best mare I ever owned, and Jessup was practically crying when he called me. He didn't even wait for my regular call, but put in a special one that night."

"Would you be any more interested if you knew that the best mare you ever owned once looked like this?"

From her purse Connie withdrew their first snapshot of Lady taken the day after she arrived at Shamrock Stables. Mr. Hill looked with distaste at the bony, battered old mare and entirely missed the hint of gentility in her pose.

"Shades of Lucifer! Look at those legs! Did you ever see such bones, or such sores? Now I'm sure it's not my Lady Be Good."

"Lady, did you say? That's the name she recognizes, Mr. Hill, honest!" Connie's conviction burned and blazed from every inch of her, but he was not warmed by it.

"My dear young lady, if I once owned every mare that has been called Lady, Hidden Hill wouldn't be big enough to hold 'em all." He took another tack. "If you own the mare now, why do you care where she came from? Whatever she's worth, you have her."

"That's a question I do not choose to answer, Mr. Hill. Look, I'm not saying that your Mr. Jessup is crooked, but someone must be. Hasn't there ever been anyone else who might have done this to Lady?"

"No!" The word crackled as their host's patience wore thin. "He has and always has had complete charge of the horses since I've owned this stable, and your whole idea is fantastic—ridiculous."

"Just say the word, Boss, and I'll give 'em the bum's rush." Grimes shifted from one foot to the other and gave Connie another idea.

"Tell me, Mr. Hill. Do you think we look like people who would want to hurt your horses? Doesn't it seem funny that Mr. Jessup should want to keep us out of here? Maybe he's trying to cover something up."

"No, I think he was just trying to save me a lot of bother. I've known him for years, and I've never seen you before. Now whose word does it seem more likely I'd believe? You're wasting your time and mine."

"Come on, Con. We might as well go." Pete had been standing behind Connie during the heated conversation, but he could now see the futility of pressing further.

" 'None so blind as those who will not see.' Next time a horse breaks a leg, better make sure it's dead, Mr. Hill," Connie flung back at him from the departing car.

"Well, it'd have been a good idea if it worked." She tried to look philosophically at Pete, but it was impossible to hide the bitter disappointment she felt. To know the truth and be so close to proving it, yet still to fail, was almost more than she could bear.

"Anyway it's only about a month now till August full moon, Connie, and then we can go back and show M. O. (these initials must mean he's from Missouri) Hill that at times even the best man's judgment wobbles. But s'posing we don't prove it—as he said, we still have Lady and her breeding."

"But, Pete, unless we can show a buyer what breeding the colts have, they won't be as interested or pay as much. And Dad said just the other day that college this fall depends on selling them.

We've put so much into improvements, we're pretty close to the wind."

"Next month'll clinch it anyway, Con."

"That's getting pretty close to the County Fair and Horse Show. If any special arrangements have to be made, there won't be much time to spare. That'll be my last-ditch stand, and everything will depend on how Shamrock Stables shows up at the Fair and Show."

"Don't bite your fingernails!" was Pete's only reply as Connie morosely stared ahead.

Pete's country days were temporarily at an end and, tarrying only long enough to pick up his stuff which had accumulated at the McGuires', he drove away. His last words were ones of encouragement to Connie, who moped like a wet chicken. True to form, when the sound of his car died away, Connie turned to the stable for comfort.

She visited Lady and the twins, but their very presence was a mockery, and her feet drifted on to Midnight and then to Dreamy. They appeared to be self-sufficient, so it was to Silver Birch, her first love, she turned for real understanding. Pushing herself up into Silver's manger, as she had done countless times before, the girl toyed with the silvery mane and whispered her troubles into the sympathetic, milk-white ear.

Even Goldy seemed to feel on the outside of the circle while the two old friends communed with each other. Slowly the realization of all the things she did have filled Connie's mind, and the thing she didn't have looked smaller than it had when she entered.

"Thanks again, Birchy. You're the best medicine for the blues I know of." She stroked the alabaster coat lovingly and lightly laid her other hand on the golden one beside it. Goldy started and rolled her eyes, but taking courage from her mother's acceptance of this creature, she suffered a few pats before she skittered off to a far corner.

To make her tour of inspection complete, Connie went into Golden Sovereign's barn. She turned to close the door after her, but whirled like a cat. What was that noise? She took two or three more steps. There it was again!

"Golden Sovereign, are you better? You aren't mean any more, and you're even nickering to me?"

She rushed toward his stall to see whether her ears were playing her tricks. No: Golden Sovereign stood in his stall, his head pressed up to the bars of the door while his nostrils ruffled an almost soundless welcome. Ears that had recently been laid flat when she approached now pricked forward eagerly, and he tossed his head as if in impatience to resume his lessons.

"Mannie, your mind's come back again. Are you cured? For good?"

She approached warily, lest he had added deceit to his other sins, but it was as though his meanness and dangerous tricks had never been. Late though it was, Connie had to find out for sure and, having crosstied him for security, she eased the bitting harness across his back and bridled him.

Still he was all sweetness and docility and, except for plenty of spirit in the ring, he behaved perfectly on the longe line. Backward and forward he went with equal ease. She changed the rope to the driving position, and though he made her puff to keep up with his long-legged stride, she loved it.

"Dad," she called to her father. "Look, Golden Sovereign's a changed horse. He's not a bit mean or spunky, and goes like a lamb. Whatever do you suppose got into him, or has gotten into him to change him back again?

"It could be more freedom," she continued. "He's been in and out of his stall without restraint since his spell began. I might have been giving him too much exercise and not enough freedom to play. After all, he's still a big baby in spite of his size."

Her doldrums over their lack of success with Mr. Hill were forgotten, and at supper Connie glowed like a firefly.

CHAPTER TWENTY

DETECTIVES
EXTRAORDINARY

THE FOLLOWING WEEKS were the happiest time of the summer for Connie. Intuition, or perhaps wishful thinking, convinced her that from the gypsies she would learn the facts about Lady Luck's change of ownership, so she gave herself entirely to the joy of working with her horses. The boarders were at the midsummer low, and there was little to keep her from the work she loved.

Golden Sovereign retained his sunny temperament day after day, and Connie at last believed that he had changed for good. She sang, she whistled, she danced through the days, with the feeling of release that comes with reconciliation after a disagreement with a dear friend. Perhaps because of the cloud that had been over him, he shone more brightly than before the dark mood came.

Connie's day began with Golden Sovereign while morning coolness was still in the air. He was either hitched to the cart or saddled, and they took to the highway for his daily dozen. In the cart he trotted tirelessly for miles on end, and under saddle they trotted and cantered more miles.

After a few weeks of it his muscles regained the hardness lost by his layoffs, and the sight of rippling skin gleaming in full sunlight was so dazzling that Connie could not refrain from laying her hand on it to feel the hidden power beneath the king's robe of gold. His dainty white feet fascinated her and his slender, clean-cut legs seemed too fragile to support him. Once she leaned over and patted a foreleg as it bowed so that his teeth might nip a juicy bit.

"I'm goofier about you than I was before, laddie. You've made me appreciate you more through your wildness than you had with your goodness. Isn't that like a woman?"

After exercising, cooling, grooming Golden Sovereign and turning him into his run, Connie turned to the other horses. She began slowly with the foals, and for days did no more than handle them and talk to them quietly. Their mothers helped as much as did her work, and it was not long before her call from the pasture gate nearly mobbed her with horses. Mares and foals came from all over to crowd and nuzzle her for a caress or some goody, and the rope she always carried soon was ignored.

The next step was to slip it around a golden neck for an instant and remove it before the youngster took fright. She continued this for many days, and toward the end she fondled their heads, rubbing lightly behind the ears and across the cheeks.

Connie's next step could not be done in a mob scene, and one by one a mare and her foal were taken into the training pasture and the little one learned about halters. Sometimes this grew lively, but through it all Connie stayed cool and patient with the youngster who was learning its ABC's.

Her afternoons were given over to the mares, who must be conditioned and groomed to perfection for their appearance at the Fair Show. Connie had not yet figured out just how she was going to get all her horses there, but she had decided that Shamrock Stables was to burst upon the public view at that time. She and her "little people" would work out details later.

Originally Connie had wanted to condition Silver and Midnight to enter in other horse-show classes, but the problem of caring for the colts and teaching them to get along for a while without their mothers at such a tender age dissuaded her. Their one and only appearance was to be in a class where they would parade and be judged with foal at side. Not only did Connie want to enter them all, to boost the Stables' name and distinction, but it would also put the foals in the limelight and possibly lure some buyers she might otherwise miss.

Days and weeks flew past like hours, and the crescent of August's new moon hung in the yellow sky above the hill. The wink of an eye later, it seemed, a half-moon illumined the farm when the sun set, and Connie's adventure was almost upon her.

Her mother and father were loath to see her and Pete go jaunting off many miles to the Thumb, and even though they had arranged for her to visit an aunt, they didn't favor the trip.

"But don't you see? I've *got* to go!" she explained without explaining at all.

"Why have you *got* to go?" her mother countered.

"It's about a horse." This seemed reason enough, but between syllables Connie decided that the time for secrecy was past, and her parents must be taken into her and Pete's schemes. "It's about Lady Luck."

"What in the world do you have to go chasing clear up there for about a horse that's already standing in your own stable? If you don't beat all!"

Connie drew a deep breath and poured out the story of McGuire and Kendall, Detectives Extraordinary, Horses a Specialty. She stressed her conviction that Lady was really Lady Be Good of Hidden Hill Stock Farm, but that the gypsies' link in the story must be established before she could confront Mr. Hill with the evidence.

"Well, Connemara, if you've got to go, I suppose you must, and I'm sure Nellie will take good care of you while you're there. But for goodness' sakes be careful when you're talking to those gypsies. I'm certainly glad you'll have Pete with you. At least I can depend on his good sense, though I can't on yours—when there's a horse in the picture anyway."

Like many before her, Connie was undecided what to wear. Slacks, however, seemed a middle ground which would fit into all the situations she would meet during her absence. She and Pete planned to leave a day before full moon, stay at Aunt Nellie's that night, and get a prompt start for the camp ground the day of full-moon night.

"Cross your fingers tight, you two. This is the climax, the pinnacle, the crux, the denouement of the whole business," she called in farewell.

Recalling Pete's remark about the possibility of bad weather, Connie scanned the sky for telltale signs and was relieved to see there was not one forerunner of storms visible. Both minds were so intent on their impending adventure that there was little conversation at first, but with so many plans to be made for Shamrock Stables' debut at the Fair Horse Show they were soon deep in arrangements.

As a child, Connie had always enjoyed her visits at Aunt Nellie's, but this trip it was no more than an unavoidable delay on the road to the gypsies' encampment. Pete gladly rose early from his temporary bed in the living room, and Connie, who had slept lightly in the guest room, was already dressed and waiting.

Her worries about the weather evaporated completely in the bright morning sunshine, and their hopes bloomed under the influence of the blue-and-gold day. Michigan's Thumb is a large piece of territory, and Pete's chance acquaintances had not been too specific about the exact location of the spot. Noon came and still they were no nearer their goal than they had been that morning.

Lunch, eaten by the roadside, was a bottle of milk and some crackers and bananas purchased at a tiny country store. Call it luck or a nudge from Connie's "little people," but she looked up as a well-filled car and trailer bearing out-of-state license plates swept past them.

"Pete, I'll bet they're gypsies coming to the pow-wow. Let's follow 'em."

"Come on then, Con." He swept up their belongings and leaped for the driver's seat and Connie banged into her place. So swift had been their reaction that the black sedan and its swarthy occupants were still in sight when they swung onto the road in pursuit. Pete stayed well to the rear, lest it annoy the leaders, but to his dismay the car had vanished after they rounded a corner. Nothing but blank road lay ahead. Cruising along slowly, they scanned the roadside for a place where so large a vehicle could have turned off. A grassy lane which cut through a break in a tall hedge had to be the answer.

Pete swerved the car into the lane, which wound across a field and into a grove that capped a knoll. A fringe of cars outlined the edge of trees, and deeper in the woods they saw many tents and campfires. Shouts of children at play came to them, and to one side they noted many horses and wagons.

"Looks as though some tribes are motorized and others stick to their traditional locomotion," Pete commented. "I suppose a car would be easier if you had to cross several states in a hurry."

It was necessary to drive to the far end of the line to park, and unsure of just what approach to use they dallied in a last-minute parley. Connie stepped out on the grass. To her surprise Pete seized her arm and sat her down forcibly on the running board while he ducked onto the floor.

"Oh, oh, Connie. Look there on the path."

She peeked as directed, and her heart dropped into the pit of her stomach. Emphasizing some statement with his finger, Todd Jessup nodded to a gypsy and strode down the path directly toward them. They tried to muffle their heartbeats, but to their relief he got into one of the nearest cars in line and, pausing only to light a cigarette, drove back down the lane, looking as if the world were his.

"He's beaten us to it. We'll never get any information out of them now—and we have only our word against his again that he was even here. Pete, it looks like we just can't win in this business." Tears were not far from Connie at this final setback to her hopes.

"It can't hurt to try," Pete resolved. "Let's go!"

He pocketed the keys to the car, and they retraced the path Jessup had just trod in triumph. They reached the brow of the knoll and were met by a swarthy man.

"What do you want?" The question, civil enough in words, implied that it was undoubtedly no good and they might as well leave.

"We'd like to talk with your leader, please."

Pete served as spokesman and Connie memorized every detail of their questioner's dress, for it seemed probable that he had been the one Todd Jessup had been talking to.

"He's busy and doesn't want to see anyone. Come back next week."

"You probably won't be here next week," Pete retorted.

"That's why I said to come back then." The gypsy smiled mirthlessly.

"Tell him, please, that Connemara McGuire wishes to ask a favor of him." She spoke with dignity and some authority. "We are not reporters or photographers, but have a personal matter to discuss with him."

She and Pete stood silent, the conversation closed. The gypsy stared at them, turning their statement over in his mind. His decision made, he gestured to them to wait and walked back to the clearing which crowned the woody knoll. He returned shortly and beckoned them on.

Without seeming to do so, Connie eyed the scene before her and tingled at the strangeness of it. Each tribe evidently had its own section, and cooking fires burned before many of the tents. Men and women lounged around the fires, and children of all ages, from tiny crawling babies to lanky youngsters, played between the trees and tents. The clearing was unoccupied except for one larger tent and preparations for what looked like a communal campfire.

Their guide stopped them before the large tent and bade them wait. He spoke a few unintelligible words at the entrance and, as if waiting just inside, a powerful middle-aged man emerged.

"Yes?" His monosyllable was less a greeting than a command to state their business and be off.

Connie drew herself up to her slim height and introduced them: "I am Connemara Anastasia Mc-Guire, and my friend is Peter Kendall. We have come to ask a favor of you." She paused, but the silence was unbroken and she continued.

"I now own a chestnut mare which several years ago a trader in Indiana bought from some of your people. I believe that some of that band is here to-day, and the favor I seek is the name or description of the man who sold that mare to them."

Her gaze was fixed on the leader, but out of the tail of her eye Connie saw the first gypsy shake his head once, emphatically. He and the leader exchanged words in a strange patois neither Connie nor Pete could understand.

"The name McGuire is an honored one in the old country, and one Shaemus McGuire many times befriended some of my people, but we have no information to give you. This man is of the tribe you mention, but he states that your chestnut mare is unknown to him."

"My great-grandfather was named Shaemus Mc-Guire. We feel only friendship for your people. This means much to me, and I beg of you to search your memories once more."

Connie knew that saying she knew they were

hiding the truth would gain her nothing. She crossed her fingers while the two gypsies conferred again.

"Regret is ours that we can give you no help. Good day."

Chagrin at being outsmarted by Jessup turned Connie's muscles limp, and her only thought was to delay their withdrawal, since that would draw a final veil across Lady's beginnings.

"Horses are my greatest interest. May we look at those you have?" She looked at a bareback horse tied to a tree nearby and gestured toward the rear, where intermittent neighs and men's shouts located the stable section.

"No, they are wild and not used to strangers. It would frighten them."

Jessup's friend spoke with authority, and it was evident that he was the head of the unmechanized division.

"Etslay us ogay. It'say ongay oodgay." Pete's pig Latin speech, meant to baffle their adversaries, snapped Connie out of her doldrums, and with a shrug of resignation she nodded.

CHAPTER TWENTY-ONE

PROOF

S CREAMS OF ALARM wheeled them in their tracks, and their faces twisted with horror. A riderless horse, reins dangling, maddened by a saddle twisted under its belly, raced toward the center of camp where the children played. The older ones scuttled for cover, but the tiny ones sprawled like leaves of the forest in the path of the insane horse.

Unmindful of their own safety, Pete and the gypsies raced toward the babies. Death or injury to some of them was certain, so scattered were they. Connie dropped her coat and purse in flight and sprinted across the clearing to the tethered horse. She undid the reins with a swift yank and flung herself onto his back. Almost before the horse's eyes snapped open from his half-doze she had kicked him into a gallop.

Dodging through the trees to meet the terrified stray, she veered to the left and burst into the path behind him. Fanning her mount with the reins and kicking him to greater efforts, she lunged abreast of the runaway just as they shot into the clearing. Connie had never played polo, but she swung her horse hard into the shoulder of the other, throwing him off stride and deflecting him from the center of the group.

No time to rejoice, for it had only aimed the maddened beast toward a solitary tot, who gurgled and waved his arms at a butterfly hovering overhead. Connie urged her mount to another burst of speed and, leaning along his neck, grabbed wildly and seized the dangling reins. She snubbed the runaway's nose down by her knee and, unmindful of the dangers of guiding two strange horses in and out through the trees, plunged into the grove.

Her left hand checked while her right held the runaway too close to allow him to charge off again. A tree slapped her left leg, missing her kneecap by a hair. Branches and small trees tore at her unprotected face, and her hands ached with their grip on the reins. Their mad flight through the woods, with the tree trunks whizzing past, dizzied her. One eye shut over a particle of bark and white-hot pains shot through her head, but she battled it out with the two horses, for the one she was riding was now drunk with speed and excitement and would have raced onward.

They roared through the grove like a small tornado, and Connie's whole mind centered on the next tree to be missed. Seconds later, though she had lived them as hours, the trees grew thinner and fell away into the grassy slope to the field.

Her last ounce of strength swerved them about in a wide circle, and the knoll's increasing steepness slowed and halted the horses.

Pete, white-faced and trembling, was in the vanguard of the men who ran to help her, and to Connie it seemed a miracle that he reached her so fast. Shaking hands seized the horses' bridles in viselike grips, and Connie knew her job was done.

"Oh-h, Pete," she whispered shakily, and slipped down in a faint.

Her eyes opened slowly, and she looked about wonderingly. She lay on a softness achieved by many folds of blankets. Above her on the tent roof, branches cast moving patches of shade. At one side sat a wrinkled old lady whose snapping black eyes and bright-colored clothes denied her age. Pete knelt on her other side, rubbing her hands and holding something aromatic to her nose.

"Hello, Pete, what's all the excitement?" she whispered.

"Connie! Thanks be, you've come to. You scared the wits out of me." His voice was shakier than hers had been.

"Am I all right?"

"Except for a few scratches and bruises, you're in better shape than I am. Phew! Was I scared! And I don't want you doing any such brainless thing again. I can't stand it." He grinned sheepishly at his show of emotion and tried to pass it off with a joke.

"Silly of me to faint."

"If you will do such things, I'm glad you had the

grace to faint and prove you're not just a super-Amazon after all. I like my gals to have a little glamour." He nodded decisively.

"Glamour doesn't have anything to do with fainting. It's just not enough blood in the brain," she said with returning vigor.

Relieved to see that she could still give him some backchat, Pete let her sit up, and her other companion nodded approvingly. At her command, a younger woman entered the tent and began applying an ointment to Connie's cuts with gentle strokes. Her eye had washed itself clean of the excruciating particle, and a pleasant tiredness made her content to lie still while her scratched face and hands and bruised leg were treated.

Connie was surprised to see a roll of antiseptic bandage pulled out and rolled around her leg. Somehow she would have expected to see a strip of medicinal bark used. But for the growing soreness of her muscles, Connie began to feel herself again and she struggled to get up.

"Wait." The old gypsy stayed Connie with a word, and she and Pete watched silently while other commands were carried out. Seven men, two of them those they had already talked to, filed into the tent and stood respectfully before them.

"I am Manya, queen of the gypsies. You came to us a stranger and were dismissed unceremoniously. Yet you risked your life to save our little ones, and proved yourself braver and a better horseman than our best." Manya flung a withering look at their first acquaintance, who wilted uncomfortably.

"We can never repay the debt we owe you, but we can grant the favor you came to us for. Speak! You have only to name it."

Connie gulped and handed her the snapshot. "That mare was sold to one of your people by someone. His name or his description is what I want."

Manya looked at the picture briefly before handing it imperiously to the men. A torrent of strange dialect accompanied the gesture and continued as the photograph went from hand to hand, ending in the reluctant grip of Jessup's friend. His jaw set stubbornly, and short, jerky sentences were spoken to the queen. She flashed back at him with a flood of abusive-sounding language.

"Jan says he doesn't know the man's name, and that he gave his word never to tell where he got the mare and to sell her in a different state." Manya flung this in an aside to Connie and Pete, who watched the proceedings with a feeling of unreality.

"Ask him if it was the man who came and talked with him today. The man with the scar?" Connie suggested softly.

Manya berated Jan vigorously and ended her tirade with some threat that made the other men start and glare menacingly at Jan. He hesitated, then nodded shortly.

"Will he write it across the back of the picture? We've got to have something besides our word."

Hardly daring to speak, lest the spell break, Connie held out Lady's snapshot.

"He cannot write. I will do it," Manya agreed grandiosely. "What do you wish me to say?"

"Say, 'This horse was sold to one of my men on [and give the date] at such-and-such a place, by a man bearing a chalk-line scar from his right temple to chin, with the promise that she would be sold out of the state.' And sign your name."

Connie expected to wake at any moment and discover it had all been a dream, but the actuality of the snapshop back in her hand proved the scene's reality. Pete hovered behind her as she rose to go and would have helped her walk, but Connie's spunk was equal to it.

"You are one of us now. Stay and join our circle about the fire tonight." Manya's voice throbbed with emotion as she offered them the hospitality of the camp.

"More than anything else I can think of, I would like to accept, but my people would be worried about me. Thank you, but we must go." The temptation to stay was almost too strong to ignore, but Connie knew her duty.

The queen of the gypsies stood up, and though the years must have been heavy on her shoulders, she was as straight and firm as anyone there. She took Connie's hand in hers and stared intently into her face.

"From this day forward all gypsies are your friends, for today you saved the lives of babies from all tribes. If you ever need help of any kind, you have but to breathe this word to a gypsy and, by Romany law, he will give his life for you if need be."

Her lips were pressed to Connie's ear and she murmured the Romany countersign. Connie nodded, but Manya was not satisfied.

"Repeat it to me." Connie complied, and Manya nodded her approval.

"Never forget. As long as there is a gypsy, and until the day you die, that word will bring you help." Manya bowed, and the seven silent men did likewise, to the retreating forms of Connie and Peter.

The swift march of events made it seem much later than it was. Connie was surprised to see the bright sunlight outside, but she welcomed the rush of air past the car. They returned to Aunt Nellie's and tarried only long enough to explain their intention to drive on home that night.

Real urgency was hot on their heels, for it was imperative to get back to Hidden Hill before Mr. Hill returned East. Possibly he had already gone, since Jessup was back on the job, but this was a chance they had to take.

Mr. and Mrs. McGuire were in bed, and the house was dark when they arrived, so it was not until breakfast that Connie's battered appearance and halting gait smote them.

"Shades of St. Patrick, girl! What have you done to yourself?" her father exploded.

"Well, I-uh, I ran through some bushes and banged my leg."

"Connemara, you're evading my question. Just what did you really do?"

As briefly as she could, Connie recounted her experience; and to distract them from laying down any future restrictions, she waved her evidence of Lady's first sale before them.

"You know what that means? That for the price of a dress I really didn't need, I've got one of the bluest-blooded saddle mares alive—when I prove with this that she is alive."

CHAPTER TWENTY-TWO

LADY BE GOOD LUCK

For the third time Connie and Pete drove toward Hidden Hill Stock Farm. Armed though they were with proof of their statements, they approached with caution. No one was about, so, easing in quietly, Pete braked the car to a noiseless halt and they hurried to the door of the big house and rang the bell.

A woman, probably the housekeeper, opened the door.

"Is Mr. Hill in?" Connie's voice squeaked nervously on the question.

"Yes, he is, but he's very busy and can't be bothered now. Is there anything I can do for you? Or can you come back again?"

"No, no, thank you. It's something personal. Could we wait out here until he's free? We've come quite a long way, and it'd be easier to stay than to come back."

Connie's keen ears had heard heavy footsteps descending the stairs, and she stalled for time. Her ruse was successful, and while the woman hesitated Mr. Hill turned the corner into the hall.

"You kids again! I thought I told you to get out and stay out. I'm too busy to be bothered with fairy tales."

"You did once, Mr. Hill, but you also said you were a businessman. I'm sure that what we have to show you will be worth one minute of your time. If it isn't, you are at liberty to bang the door."

Connie's straightforward statement stayed his hand, which had the door nearly closed. He paused and slowly swung it open again. "All right. One minute you have. Get started."

Without saying a word, Connie showed the snapshot to him and flipped it over so that he could read what was written on the back. He looked at it with momentary disbelief and reread it. Undeniably his man Jessup was mixed up in something!

"Come into my study." He stamped ahead of them and, waving them to chairs, closed the door. "All right. What's your story?"

Pete motioned that it was Connie's story, and she began with the horse auction and progressed step by step to the preceding day.

"I was sure all along that Lady had been a fine horse, but I didn't dream she'd turn out to be anything as super as your Lady Be Good," she concluded in unconscious tribute.

The room was silent, except for the tapping of Mr. Hill's fingers. Several times he turned to look at the picture again, and finally compared it with one he drew from an album on the shelf. His jaws closed with decision. Picking up the phone, he twisted the crank angrily.

"Jessup. Come to my study at once."

A rooster crowing, the whinny of a horse, the slam of a door were the only sounds in the study while they waited, and now that it was too late Connie felt a twinge of sympathy for this man she was about to strip of everything. He was a good man with horses, and she thought of Shady Lady; but that picture faded, like a double exposure, into one of Lady Luck in the auction stable, and her heart hardened to ice just as he entered.

"My young friends again. To what are we indebted for this unexpected visit, Boss?" He leered, somewhat uneasily to be sure, at the sober young people.

"To this, Jessup." Mr. Hill showed him the writing on the picture. "Start talking if you have anything to say."

"Why, that's the same picture they had before. They probably forged that stuff. Don't let 'em take you in, Boss. You're too smart an operator for that!" His hearty laugh, which didn't quite ring true, boomed out, to be replaced with righteous anger. "What are you kids up to? Coming here and trying to make trouble?"

"I don't intend to be as you call it 'taken in' by them or by you either, Jessup. Come with me. And bring a shovell!"

Mr. Hill stalked across the pasture accompanied by Jessup, who kept up a running conversation to belittle Connie and Pete and their surmises, but it was all one-sided, for the owner of Hidden Hill never spoke until they reached a spot beneath an oak. Connie had had difficulty keeping up with them because of her sore leg, and she saw Mr. Hill hesitate and look around.

"Where's that pile of rocks that used to be here? Anyway this is the place—sure, there's the mound and the stone you used for her head.— All right, Jessup; start digging. There must be something left, if it's only her shoes."

"Boss, you're letting yourself get excited over a lot of childish twaddle. Isn't my word good with you any more?"

"We'll see how good it is later. Start digging!"

Jessup thrust the shovel into the earth and worked earnestly, but his motions grew slower and slower. The shovel grated on stone. He tried another spot with the same result, then threw the shovel down.

"You win, Boss. Lady Be Good isn't here. I did sell her—but I can explain."

"Explain, can you, you rascal? You can save that for later."

He beckoned to Connie and Pete to follow him, and the procession reversed itself across the pasture. Back in his study, Mr. Hill sat down and faced them. "I am indebted to you for exposing that man. Heaven knows what else he may have falsified. Now what is it you want?"

Connie outlined her hopes and plans for Shamrock Stables, told about Golden Sovereign, showed the newspaper clipping of Lady Luck's twin palominos.

"They're good, of course, as they stand, but with their mother's pedigree behind them it'll make them that much better horses. I suppose Lady Be Good really still belongs to you, but I'd like to buy her from you if I may."

"I've heard the expression 'paying for a dead horse,' but never exactly 'buying a dead horse,' young lady." Mr. Hill smiled grimly. "Do you realize what offer for Lady Be Good I once turned down?" He named a figure that made Connie's head reel and staggered even Pete, who was accustomed to hearing his father talk big business.

"However, as I say, you may have saved me other greater losses, so I'm willing to be reasonable, and I'll give you a choice. You can keep her as she is, without papers, absolutely free. Before I could sell her as a registered mare, her identity would have to be re-established. In that case my price would have to be higher. Which do you prefer?"

Like lightning Connie's mind flashed back and forth between the alternatives as she tried to estimate what her cash resources might be, but she knew what she wanted. Her voice trembled slightly from the intensity of her feeling when she replied, "I'd still like to have her with papers, Mr. Hill, if I can meet your figure." Her eyes unconsciously blinked shut an instant as she waited for the blow to fall.

"That means you'll have to get sworn statements from every person who ever owned her, which we can file with the official registry association. Under those circumstances I feel I must ask you at least—um-m-m, shall we say one dollar?"

Connie laughed aloud with relief. "Terms or cash, Mr. Hill?"

"Terms, if you want them, young lady, plus the opportunity for me to visit Lady and admire those sensational twins of hers. What about tomorrow? I'm leaving the first of the week for the East, but I must see these horses of yours first."

Before they left, Mr. Hill handed Connie a legal bill of sale and, in case the necessary papers should not be ready before he left, instructions as to what she should do with them. The day was still young, and as their way lay through the city they elected to begin obtaining the necessary affidavits from Lady's previous city owners.

"It wouldn't be so hard if it weren't for the business of finding a notary public near each place," Pete mused. "Too bad one of us isn't one. I'll tell you—" His eyes lit with inspiration. "Let's stop at Dad's office and borrow one of his men who's a notary and take him around with us!"

"Great, if your father doesn't mind, but it probably won't look nearly as important to him as it does to us."

"It might. He's been pretty interested lately in Shamrock Stables and always asks how you're doing when I come home. We can try anyway!"

Mr. Kendall was more than willing to accommodate them, and even provided a larger car for the occasion. Once Connie's luck turned, it did it 100 percent, and by midafternoon affidavits from the sales stables and R. R. Alston nestled in her purse beside the bill of sale. For a souvenir she had kept the slip from the auction lot where she had bought Lady.

"Time for a malted milk, isn't it?" Pete's father suggested when they returned to thank him for his assistance, and though his reception room was whirring with activity, he took them to a drugstore and perched at the counter between them.

"Well, young lady, judging by Peter's reports you're pretty busy these days. Glad you keep this young fellow out of trouble too."

He looked genuinely surprised at Connie's glowing account of how helpful Pete was and what a first-class hired hand he made. "Though you can't really call him a hired hand if he does so much for free," she considered.

"How's that land next to yours working out? All right?"

"Just fine, Mr. Kendall. It has been a lifesaver to us since we've had so much more stock. Lucky for us we could get it."

"Excellent. Peter said it was well worth—what, Peter? Oh, yes, um-m, that's good—glad to know you're keeping him busy."

They left Mr. Kendall at the entrance to his factory and walked to the car.

"Connie, are your 'little people' good at hypnotism too?" Pete asked quizzically.

"What do you mean? I don't know just what the 'little people' do but be helpful. Why?"

"You may not realize it, but you have just accomplished the century's minor miracle. 'Auto Magnet Kendall pauses in midafternoon for snack with son and friend to talk farming,'" Pete declaimed, as though quoting a newspaper headline. "What is this power you have over men?" He looked searchingly at her as if to fathom her secret.

"Don't be silly. He was hungry, and maybe wanted to see more of you than your vanishing back." Connie lightly dismissed Pete's incredulity.

"All right, all right, maybe so. But it's never happened before in *my* nineteen years. Hungry, eh? That's when he chews up a mouthful of bolts and washes 'em down with lubricating oil. It beats me!"

Connie nearly wore the hides off all the horses, grooming them for Mr. Hill's visit, but her work was well worth the effort. Each coat, whether black or silver or chestnut or gold, shone like glass, and manes fluffed in the fitful summer breeze. Remembering the picture they had made in the pasture, she turned them out to add the beauty of freedom.

When she heard his car approaching, she resisted an impulse to toss a few pebbles at the horses to liven them up, but the sight of a stranger was sufficient to send the colts off across the field in a flight that curved back toward their serene mothers.

Mr. Hill removed his glasses and polished them to better scan the small but select stable, and Connie must tell him the history of each one. To Golden Sovereign he paid the highest tribute of silence before his curiosity required details.

"Superb animal. Have you broken him yet?"

"Oh yes. I've been riding or driving him for a year. Would you care to see him in action—if my bum leg holds up?"

He would, and the stallion's regal bearing was crowned with bridle and saddle. It was a scramble for Connie to hoist herself up with her sore leg, but the horse had learned his lesson well and stood motionless. Fresh from several days' layoff, Golden Sovereign put every ounce of his vitality into his movements and strutted around the paddock. At a trot, his legs snapped back and forth like pistons, and his canter had the resilience of hard rubber.

"Perfection! He's a real gold mine if he continues to sire such palominos as these. Now let's have a reunion with Lady Be Good."

Connie whistled to the mare, but all of them crowded toward her, and they had some difficulty in singling out Lady. The girl watched silently as Mr. Hill renewed acquaintance with the mare. With sorrowing eyes he noted the scars and marks of abuse that she still carried, and his brow darkened with anger.

"Lucky for Jessup I didn't see Lady before I talked to him! To think that a gentle creature who had had nothing but good care and pampering all her life should have had to bear the cruelty and misuse that she has.

"Perhaps I was too lenient with him, but he has been a good man except for this one offense. He said he needed money badly. He was in some trouble he wouldn't explain even now, and said he was afraid to ask me for a loan. Anyway, I'm keeping him on probation, and if, as he says, it was his only mistake and it never happens again, he can stay. Lady's been gone several years and I haven't caught him in anything else, so maybe he is telling the truth. We'll see."

"I'm glad," Connie said simply. "At the last minute I felt sorry for him. Then I remembered how pitiful Lady Luck was when I found her, and didn't care what happened to him.

"It's hard to remember she's really Lady Be Good. Maybe I can combine her names and call her Lady Be Good Luck, 'cause that's what she'll always be to me!"

CHAPTER TWENTY-THREE

FINAL PREPARATIONS

PETE, WITH HIS FATHER'S BLESSING, had offered to secure affidavits from Lady's distant former owners, who couldn't be reached by letter. In Connie's wildest dreams she hadn't imagined that Lady would turn out to be so well-bred, and it had not occurred to her that she would need statements to reinstate the mare.

Josephine Miller and G. J. Nolan had been most obliging and sent their affidavits almost by return mail, but Pete still had to get photostat copies of the Western Michigan Livestock Company's check stub as well as make the long trip to the "rainbow farm" near Fort Wayne.

"I might ask the gypsies to do it for me," she grinned at Pete, "but I'm sure you'll do it just as well."

Connie had been so preoccupied with the saga of Lady Luck that it was with a start she realized the County Fair and Horse Show were only three weeks distant. Not only did she have horses to prepare, but the necessary preliminary arrangements appalled her.

The advance copy of the program disclosed only one class, Mare and Foal, which the mares and colts could enter, but to show some and not all was unthinkable. Yet it would require a total of— she twiddled her fingers to count—six handlers to show them, and she could not count on Pete, for he would be showing Dreamy and would need an extra man himself. And how to transport all the horses? The County Fair grounds were not far away in miles, but too far for the young ones to hack.

Connie thought while she worked, but unable to find a solution, she combined Golden Sovereign's workout with a ride to the lake for a talk with Dr. Casey. Notwithstanding his long canter, the stallion pranced into the Laughing Horse and, trumpeting loudly, announced their arrival.

Dr. Casey greeted her warmly and invited her to alight for a chat.

"Thanks, Doc, but I can't. Smarty here is pawing the skies and needs a few more miles to unroll under him, but I've got another problem and came straight to you."

She sketched her difficulties, sure of complete understanding and, more likely than not, the perfect solution.

"For one thing I'd like to rent your van for two or three days, but what to do about the manpower shortage? I've thought of everyone—even Mom, who doesn't care to be in the limelight, as well as the girls in our old Pegasus Patrol—but none of them knows anything about showing horses that way—and it's important." She shrugged apologetically. "I don't either much, but that's my hard luck."

Doc chewed his moustache thoughtfully. "Looks like you need some professional assistance, Connemara. I'll think about it and be over sometime tomorrow to talk with you. You willing to use whoever I can find?"

"Sure enough."

"How you training those foals? You teaching them to be handled? And to pose well? And to stand still when they should?"

"I'm trying to, Doc, but it's discouraging business with a bunch of will-o'-the-wisps like they are. Tomorrow you see what you think."

Her burden had lightened already, and Connie and Golden Sovereign went on their way. His hoofs hammered out the long route home, and at its end he was cared for and Connie resumed her work with the others. One by one the foals were haltered and led around, and Connie studied their performance critically.

Their personalities had developed to a point where each was an individual and differed from the others. Goldy was a perfect little lady and as well-mannered a baby as Connie could wish. Her first coat had thinned out, and creamy gold hairs showed through the fuzz.

Dawn, though not as well-behaved as Goldy, was quick as a flash, and once Connie had made her understand she seemed to take delight in showing off her ability. Her real coat, slightly richer and deeper than Goldy's, began to hint at its appearance.

Golden Opportunity and Golden Ruler were Connie's bad pennies and acted like harum-scarum youngsters. The others' seniority was evident, for these two still seemed like balls of fuzz mounted on stilts, and "manners" was a word they found hard to understand. They were halter-broken, but what came after that didn't bother them a mite, and Connie's attempts to teach them to stand or pose might just as well have been spent on a spring breeze.

"You'll do though, my beauties. All four of you. You're too young to have developed enough to suit the judges, but I'll dazzle everyone with my little golden nuggets, and that's what I want. That's what I must have, if I'm to go to college this fall."

As Connie had expected, Dr. Casey was impatient to see the horses again and arrived soon after breakfast. From Golden Sovereign right on down to the second-born twin, Golden Opportunity, Connie put them through their paces for her friend, who watched in silence. At the conclusion of her private horse show, she looked inquiringly for his verdict.

"They're all mighty young to take any prizes. Foals that age might turn into any kind of a horse. Good ones can develop into poor horses, and some that don't look so good at this age become dandies. What is your real reason for entering them?"

Connie thought for a moment and then spoke

carefully: "I know they're young, and except for maybe a Mare and Foal Class where all the others are young too, I hardly expect to win any ribbons. *But*—and this is my reason—unless I can sell some for later delivery, college is out of the question this fall. And I want to go! I figure that this show is the place to spread Shamrock Stables' wares for horsemen to see—and want."

"Sounds reasonable, and this Fair Show answers all your requirements. Being a combination county fair and horse show it attracts breeders as well as horsemen who never intend to raise horses, and there is more variety of classes than you'd ever find in either one or the other.

"You know, Connemara, speaking of luck—which we weren't—you couldn't have picked a better part of Michigan for your grandparents to settle in than this. Do you suppose they knew that you'd be coming along and raising horses, so they just plopped down here in what was to be the middle of the horsiest part of the state?"

"Oh, I'm sure they did," Connie agreed dryly. "And no doubt they built beside a lake because they knew I'd like to swim."

"Well, as I was saying before your grandparents interrupted me, you've picked the perfect place to launch Shamrock Stables' golden horses, and I can loan you the handlers you need. What classes do you plan to enter?"

"Don't know for sure. In the livestock section I thought Mare and Foal for all of them, Produce of Dam for Lady (I'd intended entering all the mares, but find it requires two or more foals), and Junior Stallion and Get of Sire for Golden Sovereign. None of the mares is in condition for any of the regular horse-show classes, but I'll enter him in every one I can. The more people see him the better they'll remember Shamrock Stables, and the stallion is the foundation of a stable. What do you think?"

"That's all right, but I'd suggest you enter Silver and Midnight in the Model Class. It's judged on conformation and type rather than performance, which shouldn't be hard on them, and you might win something. They're mighty fine mares, but poor old Lady is too banged up."

Pete's arrival interrupted their conference, but he proved the success of his trip by handing over the prized affidavits. They reconvened with him as extra consultant, as well as a rival in the Mare and Foal Class.

"I've already got somebody to help me with Dreamy and Golden Music in that class," he stated triumphantly. "Guess who?"

"Give up. Who is it?"

"My dad! Imagine: I was worrying about who to get, as I knew you'd have no time, and if he didn't ask me if he could do it! What's more, he and Mother are coming out Sunday so he can practice. I don't know whether I'm going crazy or he is!"

Mr. and Mrs. Kendall enjoyed their visit so thoroughly that they returned several times, to Pete's utter bewilderment.

"Dad's putting history into a tailspin. Instead of

man turning to autos from horses, he's turning to horses from autos. It's phenomenal, and he seems to enjoy it. Mother too. She even asked me the other day if I thought it'd be hard for her to learn to ride," Pete confided to Connie after they left.

Connie bided her time and casually suggested to Mrs. Kendall later, "Wouldn't you like to ride Lady around the paddock a little while? It'd do her good."

Mrs. Kendall demurred, but at Connie's guarantee of Lady's good manners and gentle disposition she succumbed. The world looked like a different place viewed from the back of a horse, and she was so entranced with riding it looked as if Mr. Kendall might soon be buying another horse. Thereafter no visit was complete for her unless Lady were saddled and bridled, and sedately ridden around the paddock.

From then until the day before the Show, Connie lived only for her horses. Work, groom, train—work, groom, train. She was too close to them herself to note any improvement, but others like Doc and Pete, who weren't with the horses all day every day, were highly complimentary about the results.

"How's Golden Sovereign been acting lately, Connemara? Any signs of that meanness he showed for a while?" Dr. Casey inquired.

"Not a bit. He's been as sunny as a day is long. I guess his spells were just coltishness and he's outgrown them."

The barns and paddocks became practically the McGuires' living room, and everyone spent the majority of his time there preparing for the big event which suddenly was only the day after tomorrow.

A temporary sign had been prepared to tack on the side of the horse van, so that all might know it contained horses from Shamrock Stables, home of Golden Sovereign, and Connie nearly burst with pride to see it in print for everyone to read. The McGuires had decided that, to save all the last-minute rush early on show day, the horses should be taken over the previous afternoon, and even with Doc's van this meant two trips.

Mr. McGuire had been elected to stay with them during the night, Connemara taking care of the farm chores night and morning, and driving over with her mother in time for their first entry.

The last day passed in a whirl for Connie, who was bathing, trimming, brushing, combing horses in such rapid succession she could hardly keep track of which one she was working on. As long as the colors were different it wasn't too hard, but once she turned to the golden foals she'd be apologizing to Goldy for an indignity she was working on Dawn. But somehow she found time to give Golden Sovereign a final sprint.

Not only were the horses thoroughly groomed, but all the tack must be given a last rubdown. It had to be counted and each class carefully thought through in advance, to make certain that no essential item was left behind.

"Jiminy, now's a time when I could certainly use several brothers and sisters," she exclaimed fervently. "Times like these, there's nothing like a big family to help out."

She and her mother and father, Pete, and even Doc, who had brought the van over early, scurried like mad to perfect their preparations down to the last rope, and before Connie felt that she was half through it was time to start with the first load. The loading ramp was lowered, and two by two, like animals in the Ark, mare and foal were led in.

The second load departed without incident, and Connie followed along in the car to do a little reconnoitering for the morrow. The stalls, she was glad to find, were roomy and comfortable, and an abundance of fresh straw was available. She prowled around the stables, peering at other early arrivals for possible champions, and though she had seen the ring many times before she tasted a preliminary thrill by walking out onto the grassy enclosure. In imagination she could see her horses lined up there, blue ribbons fluttering from every bridle.

"On behalf of Shamrock Stables, it gives me great pleasure to accept the grand championship, and may I add that each year we hope to be represented here by finer and finer horses. Thank you." Ringing applause greeted her statement and jarred her out of her rosy dreams. To her chagrin it was only Pete leaning out of the center box.

The task of doing the farm chores that evening seemed too tame for one who, on the following day, would have the acclaim of multitudes ringing in her ears, but the animals left behind had to be fed and cared for. The barn was so lonesome with all her darlings gone she could hardly bear to enter it.

A forlorn bleat near Golden Sovereign's stall attracted her attention, and she was full of remorse that Camellia had been left alone.

"Come along, girlie, we'll put you in the cows' part tonight so you'll have a little company. Pretty quiet in there with just your own thoughts, isn't it?"

With completion of the chores Connie's work was not yet finished, for then there was the problem of getting herself ready. Boots had to be shined until they glistened like polished oak; her hair had to be fixed to her satisfaction, and clothes for the morrow laid out for a lightning change after morning chores. Small wonder that it seemed she fell into a deep sleep while her head was still a couple of inches above the pillow.

CHAPTER TWENTY-FOUR

SCRATCHED!

Between waking and finding herself entering the ring with Lady in the Produce of Dam Class, there seemed to be no more than a heartbeat, and Connie would not have been too surprised to find she was still in pajamas. She was not, however, and nightwear had somehow been exchanged for trim riding clothes.

Lady Be Good Luck behaved like the veteran she was at horse shows, and after the entrants had paraded around the ring, Connie, her father, and Pete lined up mare and twins. They created quite a stir in the well-filled stands, and hand clapping followed them around.

All the other mares had more than two foals

with them, and in each case their ages were considerably greater than Lady's two babies. Connie had to concede that there were some superb animals against her—animals that were no better than Lady, but whose years had been easier and had left no scars with their passing.

"Here come the judges. Get set!" she called *sotto voce* to the others, who were doing their best to keep the madcap youngsters posed.

She vibrated Lady's lead rein and clucked to her softly. The mare responded by arching her neck a trifle more, and her tail fairly quivered with her effort at stylish carriage. All four legs stretched out at an angle from her body as she tried to recapture the beauty and style that had won for her on other occasions.

The judges squinted at her from every angle, repeating the performance with each foal, and walked slowly around them singly and as a group. Connie's hopes rose to see their heads nod in agreement, but declined as they talked animatedly for a while. They turned to Connie.

"Which Lady Be Good is this? A famous mare of that name died several years ago—or was destroyed."

"This is that one," Connie said, to their mystification, but hurried on. "She wasn't really shot, but only thought to be. Instead she was spirited away, and I bought her about eighteen months ago at an auction yard. Since then I have traced her back, and I have here a letter establishing the fact that this is in fact Lady Be Good of Hidden Hill."

They listened like little boys to a fairy story, asked a few more questions, and passed on to the next entry. For the remainder of the class Connie tried to decide whether Lady's story would help or harm her chances, but the loud-speaker settled it. One of the judges spoke, and to Connie's disbelieving ears announced that Shamrock Stables had taken first prize.

"After careful deliberation we have decided that the award in this class must recognize not only the unusual character of the entry—twins— but also the inherent qualities of the mare which at present, to be sure, are not too visible," and he briefly outlined Lady's story.

Walking on top of the world, Connie led Lady forward to receive the blue ribbon while the foals seemed to caper with joy. The thrill of her first victory was made the sweeter by having several people stop at the stalls to see the foals.

"Any of these for sale?" one inquired.

"They're too little to separate yet, but I'd be willing to consider selling them now for delivery later." Connie's mind was in a turmoil, wondering just how high a price she dared ask for each. She knew the horse market well enough to know that the prized golden color added many dollars to the value of a horse, however good.

"I may be back again then after we see how the sire stacks up with the other stallions shown," came the reply, and Connie felt like a burst balloon.

Connie went to Golden Sovereign's stall to impress upon him the importance of a good showing when his turn came. Far from understanding the burden which rested on him, his eyeballs rolled ominously, and one hind foot flashed out and thudded against the rear wall.

"Sliver!" she snapped sharply. "Don't you go getting any smarty ideas now. If ever I'm depending on your good behavior, it's now, and I don't want any nonsense."

He stared sulkily at her, and though to a stranger his manner might not seem at all bad, a shiver of apprehension went up and down Connie's spine.

"Oh, you're just rarin' to go, fellow. You'll feel all right soon as you get a chance to strut your stuff in front of all the people—I hope!"

She welcomed the bustle of preparing the mares and foals for Shamrock Stables' mob scene in the Mare and Foal Class. Doc and his extra men were on hand, and it looked like a parade when they started for the ring: Connie leading Midnight, her father with Silver, Doc leading Lady, Pete with Dreamy, and his father and the other men following each mare with her cloth-of-gold foal.

A hum of appreciation greeted their entrance into the ring, and truly Shamrock Stables held the limelight, for nearly half of all the foals entered in the class had been sired by Golden Sovereign. The mares stepped along quietly, turning their heads occasionally to be sure that their precious young ones were close behind. Round and round they went while the judges stood in the center, scanning one group after another, and Connie began to feel that they themselves were being judged on conformation and manner of going.

No one needed a second command to line up in the center, and Connie, who could see that the judges were impressed by her mares, grew more and more tense as the fatal moment of decision neared. With fine-tooth combs each mare and foal was examined by the sober judges.

They went into a huddle over their scoring boards, and the girl's heart thumped so uncomfortably and her breathing was so irregular she couldn't have cheered the results had she dared. Midnight's number was called first, followed by Dreamy's, an outsider's, and Silver's. Two ribbons out of four—almost three, since Pete's Dreamy was related at least by marriage!

Had she won no ribbons at all, Connie would have considered her entry in the class worth while on account of the stir created by the parade of palominos. But ribbons too!

Visitors really began to seek them out in earnest, and someone from Shamrock Stables had to be ready to answer all kinds of questions about the stables and its horses. Connie was a little disappointed, though she would not admit it, that no one had actually gotten down to business on the matter of buying any of the foals. Many of the callers had looked at Golden Sovereign from a distance, but afraid that too many strangers might upset him, she had had to defer their interest by suggesting that they observe him in action.

The show had been arranged to have the livestock classes in the mornings and the usual horse show during the afternoon sessions, when more spectators would be present. This suited Connie, for it meant that Golden Sovereign would get a good workout before his appearance the next morning in the stallion classes.

She had entered him in as many classes as possible, but there were three or four in which she had hopes of placing. The lunches Mrs. McGuire had put up that morning were supplemented by soft drinks from a stand, in spite of her mother's dire warnings that no good would come of putting that stuff in their stomachs, and they turned to putting the finishing touches to Golden Sovereign for his innings.

His rolling eye had truly forecast an approaching storm, and the four of them had their hands full getting him saddled for the Three-gaited Class. Connie was glad that this came first, as he was full of fire and ginger, which would improve his style and his chances of winning.

The loud-speaker blared the announcement that entries in the Three-gaited Class were riding into the ring, and Connie joined the others. The noise and motion reacted as always on the stallion, and he pranced in on tiptoe. To others he looked like just a spirited horse full of fire and beauty, but his rider could feel the tightness of his muscles, and she prayed for a hard workout which would dull the edge of his temper somewhat.

At a wave from the judges, horses and riders

swept forward in a trot, and Connie forgot her forebodings in the perfection of his stride. Like an automaton his legs flashed forward and back, forward and back, and his hoofs seemed to disdain the ordinary earth and to tread on clouds. She was not unmindful of the picture they made, his glowing coat enriched by the afternoon sunlight which tipped his mane and tail with light as they whipped in the breeze.

A walk, and a canter, and they reversed. There followed more trots, walks, canters, trots than Connie could keep track of with all her faculties concentrated on getting the most from her mount. His flare-up of temper served to increase his action and style, and for once Connie was not sorry, but in the back of her mind a termite of worry bored constantly to remind her of how far his bad spells could carry him.

There were other handsome high-stepping horses present, however, and a third-place ribbon fell to her.

"That's fine, Connemara," Dr. Casey said in congratulation. "Just a little different shoeing might make the difference between third and first—or even what the judge ate for lunch."

"I'm satisfied with third today, Doc. He felt like coiled steel, and I'm thrilled that he placed at all."

One class intervened before Golden Sovereign was scheduled for the Combination Class for harness and saddle horses. Connie had at first demurred from entering in this class on the grounds that their cart was not stylish enough, but Doc had insisted.

"You want to show your horse, don't you, and to prove his versatility? Then this is another way to do it. He looks superb in harness—and a lot of them don't, for a saddle can cover a lot of faults. With just a few straps across a horse, he's right out there for the judges to see every inch of him, and some just can't stand it as well as he can. Trust a woman to worry about what she or the horse is going to wear!"

The Three-gaited class workout had not sweetened Golden Sovereign up any, and hitching him to the cart was a two-fisted job. Connie cast a wary glance at his back feet when she stepped into the cart and took the reins Doc held out to her.

"Don't worry, Connemara. We'll be standing by for the time you have to unhitch and change to a saddle. Just drive him for all he's got, and he'll forget that nonsense that's gotten into him."

The class began smoothly enough with several circuits of the ring at a walk. This enabled her to cast an appraising eye at her opponents and their horses, and she honestly felt that Golden Sovereign outclassed them all.

"Trot," crackled in the air and she sent him on until the spokes of the wheels flashed and blended into a single blur of motion. "So far, so good," she thought, but too soon. Golden Sovereign wasn't content with a spanking trot and broke into a canter, the height of bad manners for a driving horse.

She pulled him down instantly, but noted a judge's pencil busy with the score pad. His first break felt so good, the stallion picked up his feet in another canter; nor was he so willing to give it up again, and nothing but the command to reverse and walk saved her from a battle. She tried to soothe the restive stallion with a flow of conversation, but he had decided he didn't want to be good, and no amount of talk was going to change him.

The next order to trot was obeyed just long enough for him to work himself into a canter from which he was anxious to go on to a gallop. Her father, Doc, and Pete watched anxiously from their positions by the fence, and their knowing eyes could recognize all the old symptoms over again. Their fingers unconsciously clinched and loosened with Connie's, and she played the horse like a fish on a line.

"Had we better suggest she leave instead of finishing the class?" Doc questioned excitedly, feeling responsible for her being in this class.

"She'd never do it," Mr. McGuire doubted. "Once she gets hold of something, she hangs on like Old Harry. All I hope is that he isn't too confounded cantankerous when we have to change over."

Golden Sovereign acted as though he were taking orders only from himself, and trotted or cantered to suit his fancy, in spite of Connie's heroic efforts to calm him.

To their astonishment, Connie drove to the gate

when the judges called for the change-over. "No use showing his faults in front of everyone. We've already lost any chance of winning anything. The cantankerous old beast!"

They stared openmouthed at the first uncomplimentary words Connie had ever directed at this apple of her eye and judged her disappointment accordingly. One walked on each side of the cart just in case the stallion made any trouble on the way back to the stables, but it was accomplished safely. Not so the unhitching, as his hoofs were much too light for the safety of anyone working around him, and only crossties protected them from his teeth.

Connie hunched on a bale of straw so engulfed by misery over the reoccurence of Golden Sovereign's dark mood that she completely forgot she was slated to ride him again that afternoon. A kindly acquaintance came running to remind her that the ringmaster was calling for them.

"Just tell 'em he's been scratched." At his look of surprise, she elaborated. "We've decided he's not in proper condition."

"That's a masterful evasion," Pete commented. "You aren't going to withdraw him from all the rest of the classes, are you? Tomorrow too?"

"I don't know for sure. Hope not. Pete, what time are the trotting races over?"

"Sometime late in the afternoon. Why?"

"Exhibitors are entitled to use the track for exercise before and after the races. If you people will be willing to go through all this again, I'm

going to take our fine friend down there this afternoon and work the socks off him. I don't know
whether it'll help any, but it can't hurt him—he's
in such a frenzy now, and getting worse."

The grandstand had emptied, and the trotters
and their handlers had returned to their stalls
when Connie and Golden Sovereign rode onto the
track. The stallion had not been easy to saddle,
and Connie's jaw was set in a way that boded no
good for him. No warm-up was necessary after his
afternoon's antics, and Connie put him into a trot.
This didn't seem to use up his energies fast enough
to suit her, and she stepped him up to a canter.

She had passed her audience of three several
times when Dr. Casey motioned her in. "Don't
you think that's enough, Connemara? He's got to
have strength enough to stand up tomorrow, you
know."

"This is only the beginning for him, Doc. He
can canter for miles. See, he's hardly breathing hard
at all and is still full of prunes."

"Once more than, and step him up a little more,
but that really ought to be all he needs, if
exercise'll cure him."

Connie walked the horse for a few rods and
then touched him up. They whirled around the
track and drew rein again by the gate where they
had entered.

"He's kind of speedy at that, isn't he?" Doc
commented. "Wouldn't think he'd know how with
his saddlebred heritage."

"He's still half Arabian, and that makes him a

distant cousin of the Thoroughbred," Connie retorted. "That Arabian blood may account for his stamina, 'cause he never seems to get tired. Look at him even now," she finished in disgust.

Certainly the exercise hadn't calmed him a bit; rather it seemed to have aroused the worst in him, for he danced and snorted and laid back his ears so that Connie was reminded of Midnight at her worst. He was so troublesome she thought it would serve him right to let him sleep in his tight saddle, but by careful handling it was removed after he had cooled, and he was sketchily groomed.

Connie banged the stall door shut on his meanness. "I don't envy you tonight, Dad. I just hope he doesn't decide to tear the place down, board by board, before morning."

CHAPTER TWENTY-FIVE

FREE-FOR-ALL

CONNIE RETURNED TO THE FARM, but her thoughts
stayed at the fairgrounds with her father and
Golden Sovereign, on whom rested the plans and
work she had done for Shamrock Stables for years.
If he went bad for keeps, none of the foals would
be salable at prices which would help her with
college, and it would mean the loss of several
years. Golden Ruler would not be ready to take the
place as herd sire for a long time, and there was
always the danger that he might turn mean as his
father before him had.

These doleful thoughts and many others paraded
through Connie's mind, and she felt a deep pang
over the prospect of not leaving for college when
Pete did that fall. To stay out one year by choice
was not hard, but to feel that going at all was
impossible was not pleasant to face.

Many wild plans and hopes flashed into her head
between leaving at night and returning the following morning, but she was levelheaded enough to
realize that they were wildly impractical. Her

first words on meeting her father drove straight to the point.

"How's Golden Sovereign? Was he as mean as ever during the night?"

"That he was, and more so." Sorry as he felt for his daughter, Mr. McGuire knew that words would not help and she would have to face trouble squarely. "Not so much during the night, but it was all my life was worth to feed him and water him last night and this morning. He has either a special hatred for me, or he's turned killer."

"Killer" rang in Connie's ears long after her father's voice had died away, and Shamrock Stables began to look like a child's dream of "when I grow up." She felt her father's eyes on her, and she squared her shoulders.

"Let's give him just one more trial, Dad. We'll scratch him from the Junior Stallion Class, but if he could just get any ribbon in Get of Sire, the foals might sell all right after all."

"Are you serious, Connemara? I wonder if you really understand just how bad he is. Why not sell him for whatever we can get and start over? There's surely some horseman here who'd be willing to fight it out with such a beauty, but we can't. If we try to show him today, he's apt to snap somebody's arm off or strike one of us down. He's wild as a range stallion that's never had a hand on him."

"Please, let's wait a bit. No one knows any better than I just how mean he can get, but it's our last chance to make something out of all the work we've done—the new barn, the extra land, everything. Let's ask Doc. He can give us a few tricks that'll help keep Golden Sovereign under control."

A council of war was held among the Shamrock Stables delegates, and since the others sided with Connie and felt that one last-straw attempt should be made, Mr. McGuire pushed his foreboding behind him. Almost behind him, for the prospect of what one wild, mean stallion could do in a ring full of other stallions and foals was appalling.

The one point no one could agree on was who was to lead Golden Sovereign for the class. Doc said that he should because he had worked with horses more than any of them. Pete maintained that it was his place since he was younger and spryer than the other men. Mr. McGuire vetoed both of them by saying that there was no use endangering themselves and that the stallion knew him better than he did them. Connie, however, ended it all by pointing out that she answered all the arguments but Doc's and that *she* was going to do it. The three men looked at each other in consternation, but nothing they said could sway her.

"After all, if it's strength you're counting on, Golden Sovereign is stronger than all of us put together, so it's the person who has trained and ridden him he'll obey if he will anyone. And that's me. Now let's decide our course of action!"

The Get of Sire Class was just before lunch, but Connie moped around the stables, refusing to accept anyone's invitation to go up to the ring and watch the morning's program. She slumped on her favorite bale of straw and brooded about her chances of keeping Golden Sovereign subdued long enough to win something and pull the stables out of utter defeat.

She looked up in surprise to see them converging on the stall, only to realize that her time of trial had come. Fortunately they had plenty of time to get ready, for Golden Sovereign resented every move they made. After much dodging and struggling, he was bridled and crosstied to permit them to curry him thoroughly.

"No matter how blackhearted he is, at least he'll look beautiful outside," Connie vowed, and beautiful he was after the grooming.

In addition to his bridle, a nose strap which might have been a cavesson had been fitted snugly around his jaw to prevent him from biting. Nothing could be done about his feet, however, and Connie's only insurance was her caution and nimbleness. The little procession of regal palomino stallion and his golden foals, who looked as if they might have been cut from the same piece of goods, headed for the ring after the loud-speaker announced that horses were then entering.

The strange sights and sounds distracted Golden Sovereign briefly, and the trip was made without mishap in spite of his one attempt to strike a passing horse. At the gate, a bit of Connie's school-day Latin flashed into her mind, and she muttered, "Abandon hope, all ye who enter here." Six other stallions preceded them into the arena, and she saw to it that plenty of space separated them.

Her hopes were pinned on a short class and a quick decision. They paraded around the ring with some difficulty, inasmuch as Golden Sovereign repeatedly paused to neigh his most insulting challenges at the other stallions. Once or twice he stopped to paw the ground as evidence of what a terror he was, but Connie flicked him on with the tip of her training whip.

As if to deliberately show off to the grandstand, he reared on his hind legs directly before it. His hoofs double-thudded to earth, and he bounced stiff-legged for an extra flourish. Every person in the stands was fascinated by his wild beauty, and the judges also watched him, but warily. The other horses' owners were made uneasy by his antics; nor was Connie exactly enjoying them.

They lined up in the center, each horse flanked by his foals, but only Golden Sovereign's were all young ones. The others' varied from young foals to yearlings and two- and three-year-olds. That didn't bother him, and while the others stood he pawed and pranced to be free. Connie's face glistened with perspiration, partly from her exertions to keep him under control and partly from nervousness lest he get unmanageable.

The judges worked their way along the line, carefully examining and evaluating the relative merits of the entrants, and just as Connie dared to hope she might still succeed Golden Sovereign went to pieces. He lunged toward the stallion nearest him, and when Connie's pull on the reins checked him, he squealed angrily. A forefoot struck out at her, but she cut it sharply with her whip.

From there on it was just a blur to Connie, who matched her wits and skill against the horse's weight and wickedness. Others would have rushed in to help her, but there seemed no opening, and they circled and dodged in a world of their own.

Seconds ticked past, and after the first shouts of alarm the only sounds were the thud of hoofs and Connie's shouted commands, which the stallion disregarded. Golden Sovereign ended the first round with an instant's pause to gather himself for a fresh outbreak, but Connie was too quick for him.

She flashed in, grabbed a handful of mane and vaulted onto him bareback. She leaned over his shoulder to sweep the reins into each hand and knew at last that she had gained the driver's seat and some degree of control, which had been impossible from the ground. Before he could launch himself into another frenzy, she cut him with the whip and he leaped forward in motion.

The gate swung open before them, and with the stallion reined down tightly they retraced the path they had covered such a short time before. There was an almost audible sigh of relief from the on-lookers as they expelled their tightly held breaths, followed by a storm of applause for the girl who had fought it out rather than turn him loose to do the damage he wished. To Connie it meant the end, since the cheers were for her, rather than for the horse.

Leaving others, any others, to hold the deserted

foals, her father, Doc, and Pete raced to the stable, but the latter got there first. Golden Sovereign's stall door was shut and Connie lay face down on the straw bale, crying bitterly.

"Con, Con, are you hurt? What happened? What's the matter?" he cried in alarm.

"What d'ya think's the matter? He disgraced the whole stable, and nobody'll ever buy one of his foals. No, I'm not hurt," she answered the alarm in Pete's voice, "but it was awful. I'll never be able to face any of those people again."

"Sure you will, Connemara. Everybody has a horse that misbehaves now and then, but there isn't a person there, man or woman, who could have done what you just did. You can look 'em all in the eye any day and know that you're a better horseman than anyone there today!"

"How'd you get him into his stall by yourself?" Doc asked breathlessly, still panting after his dash from the ring.

"I just rode him up to the doorway, slipped off, and clapped the door shut behind him. He's still got his best bridle on, and it'll probably be torn to bits. But I don't care!"

Lunchtime was a mournful affair for them, and Connie was all for packing up and leaving at once, but she was reminded of the Model Mares Class in which she had entered Silver Birch and Midnight Moon.

"What's the use! Golden Sovereign has put his foot right through the center of everything. Why keep on struggling?"

Such an attitude was so alien to Connemara that the others were unwilling to have her leave on that note, and they united to cheer her up. "But you can prove that Shamrock Stables has good mares. Just because Golden Sovereign is no good you should show what good mares you have, and that might help just as much," each of them argued in a different way.

Halfheartedly Connie agreed to stay long enough for that class. Just as they had hoped, it was impossible for Connie to work around a horse without being comforted, and some of her old sparkle had returned by the time the silver and black mares were led into the ring.

Everyone recognized her, of course, and such a tumult of applause had never been heard before as that which went up when the blue ribbon was pinned to Midnight's bridle. But it was only a whisper compared with the shout of approval at the judges' awarding second-place ribbon to Silver.

Connie's head was up and her step springy with new hope when she left the ring, but back at the stalls fresh misery swept over her. No college, no stables, no nothing. The future stretched drearily ahead, and her recent triumph with the mares made it worse since she knew that her stock was excellent.

Listlessly she busied herself with collecting and packing the tack and equipment for an ignominious retreat. A few days before she would have scoffed had anyone told her she'd be leaving a day early and before Golden Sovereign had kinged it over the next day's classes, but everything was changed. She banged a brush into a box in a burst of futile anger.

Pete skidded around the corner, grabbed a post to check his flight, and sank down out of breath. "Sorry to stay away so long, Con. I've been down by the track listening to some fellows argue about trotting horses and running horses, and I forgot it was so late. One of 'em is bragging about his red horse—says trotting races are child's play. Thought for a while they'd get into a real fight."

"It's a wonder they didn't. Harness men are pretty keen about it. Who's the smart aleck?"

"Didn't know him. He's a terrible loudmouth—says he'll back his red horse against all comers in a two-mile free-for-all. It looked as though he'd find some takers too. Let's come back to watch tomorrow, if it comes off. It may not though; he's setting the stakes pretty high and winner take all, so I guess he knows pretty well what his horse can do."

"How much is he willing to stake on it?" Connie asked, and new lights danced in the back of her eyes.

She whistled softly at the figure Pete gave, but her packing grew slower and slower while she listened to Pete's description of the encounter. She slammed the lid of the tack box shut. "Let's go back and listen. Sounds interesting!"

It was not difficult to locate the braggart at the core of a group into which Connie elbowed her way. The argument had grown more heated during Pete's brief absence, but evidently no one had called the man's bluff, for he continued to swagger about.

"How do you know you could use the track?" a voice taunted.

"My good man, it's always possible to arrange a special match which would be of interest to the spectators. And a sporting event between gentlemen has the thrill of the professional with the charm of the amateur. But I guess there are no sportsmen present, or is it no horsemen?"

Across from Connie was a man whose face grew purpler by the minute. His mouth sagged open several times, but he made no sound until the final jibe.

"You probably feel pretty sure of yourself and your horse, Coleman, but I'm just the man who thinks he can make you eat crow. Count me in."

Connie's mind was in a turmoil. Here was a second chance to snatch victory out of defeat and still get to college. Like a movie her mind flashed back to Golden Sovereign's tremendous stamina and his effortless gallops for miles. Dared she take such a chance?

"Would you accept a prize palomino filly as an entry fee?"

Everyone looked at her in amazement, and she felt as though she too were staring at this girl who had spoken.

"Well, well, so it's ladies' day too?" Coleman turned and was astonished to see a slender young girl.

"All right with me, but a race is no child's play, you know. I'll leave the decision about your stake to the other gentleman, since he's so sure his horse will win."

Two others who had teetered on the brink of entering were pushed in by seeing a girl take the step. In all there would be a field of five horses in the race and, as if she had already won it, Connie calculated that the purse would give her a comfortable margin for college. Track officials were contacted, and they readily agreed to arrange the special match to precede Saturday afternoon's trotting program.

No one had been more stunned than Pete when Connie had so blithely entered, and as they walked to the stables he tried vainly to dissuade her.

"But Pete, it's not often that opportunity knocks twice, and here's my chance to make up for all the damage Golden Sovereign has done. It won't make him any better as a sire of foals, but at least I'll make something off him."

"You will if he doesn't bolt the other way—or take off across the infield. He isn't exactly to be depended on, you know."

"I just hope he doesn't remember what a jumper his mother was when she was a girl," Connie admitted ruefully. "If I can just keep him on the track, headed the right way, I think we stand a chance—"

"And if you don't get your neck broken, you'll live to enjoy your college career—if you don't get some other harebrained notion."

News traveled fast, and Mr. McGuire descended on the stable from one side as Dr. Casey did from the other. Connie's father said flatly it was sheer nonsense and he would not permit her to go ahead with the plans until he had talked with her mother. Connie never knew just what they said in this parental conference, but he returned with their grudging consent and his opinion that it would at least get rid of one foal. Doc, remembering Golden Sovereign's performance on the track the evening before, rubbed his chin and allowed that he might give the other horses a run for their money.

They began speculating on Golden Sovereign's chances of winning and what to do to prepare him for the ordeal. Ordeal it would be, too, for a mile race is long enough to test the heart and courage of any horse, and two miles grinds him down to the last drop of stamina.

"If only he'd calm down enough to get a decent night's rest, but I suppose he'll bang around as usual," she mourned. "Why did he have to have this mean spell now? But then if he hadn't, he'd have won in the show and I wouldn't even have been tempted to enter this free-for-all."

They decided to leave him in his stall until morning, give him a short breeze to warm him up, and hope that he'd be fit for the race and manageable enough to saddle and head in the right direction. The latter seemed highly improbable, however, as his temper had gone from bad to worse and he hated everyone and everything.

CHAPTER TWENTY-SIX

WINNER TAKE ALL

Every ounce of weight was important, and Connie got out the tiny racing saddle she had been given years before and checked its girths and stirrups. Her own clothes were considered carefully from the standpoint of weight, and she chose her softest, lightest pair of boots. Mrs. McGuire was deeply concerned over the whole affair, but before Connie left for the fairgrounds in the morning, her mother handed her a green-silk blouse on which she had sewed a broad band of yellow ribbon.

"Kelly green and gold ought to be lucky for Shamrock Stables, and St. Patrick himself knows you'll be needing luck."

Connie's hug expressed her appreciation, and she faced the day more confidently than she knew she had any right to. Doc and her father met her with long faces by Golden Sovereign's stall.

"Connemara, we're not sure we'll ever be able to get this brute saddled. He's meaner'n a rattlesnake this morning, and what you'll ever do with him in a race is beyond us. Well, let's try again!"

By getting a rope around his neck and through into the next stall, his head and neck were held to the wall long enough for Connie to slip in, bridle, and crosstie him. That checked him sufficiently for them to complete the saddling; then Connie, her heart beating like a muffled drum, mounted. As soon as he felt the track under him, Golden Sovereign wanted to race with the wind, and the girl thanked fortune that his mouth was soft enough for her to control him.

The workout was short—just enough to limber his muscles and whet his desire for more. In his stall again, the stallion tore around without ceasing.

"He's running his race now, I'm afraid," Doc lamented. "He'll be burned out by the time he hits the track and will only lope around and eat dust. If we could only quiet him down some way, but short of hitting him on the head I don't know what would work!"

Pete went off to scout the other horses, and on his return it was unnecessary to ask his opinion. His dejected manner and "it-won't-hurt-to-try" attitude was eloquent tribute to Golden Sovereign's opponents. The minutes ticked past into hours, the race came closer and closer, and the section by the stallion's stall had all the appearance of an Irish wake.

Tiring of inaction, Doc and Mr. McGuire strolled toward the center of excitement and left Connie and Pete slouched on their respective bales. They looked up from time to time at exhibitors who were taking their stock out early, but a procession of the world's heroes since Alexander the Great would have stirred Connie but little.

Suddenly Golden Sovereign's neigh pealed out so sharply that Connie jumped, expecting to see him bearing down on her. His hoofs thundered on the walls and his shrill whinnies continued, occasionally softening to a tender huh-huh-huh which contrasted strangely with his apparent rage.

Connie rushed to the stall to see what had touched him off, but no solution offered itself. Concluding it was just a burst of temper, she returned to her seat and noticed some of the goat entries walking past. In her head a warning bell jangled, and she struggled to fit the pieces of her mental jigsaw puzzle together: Golden Sovereign's lonesome huh-huh-huh, goats, dark moods—

"Pete, Pete. That's it! I've got it!" Almost too excited to talk, Connie babbled her discovery. "He's lonesome for Camellia. She's always been in the stall next to him. Every time he's gone sour, they've been apart: that first time I left him to be shod; when he stayed overnight at the Marchland's Show; the times her owners took her away; and now because we didn't bring her. She's his mascot, and he thinks he's lost her."

Startled out of his doze, first by Golden Sovereign's outburst and then by Connie's shout of discovery, Pete had trouble catching up with her, but as she flung out half-sentences and phrases of exclamation he leaped up excitedly. "Connie, you're right! Every time that's been the way."

He was running for his car before he finished speaking, and a quick glance at his watch made him spurt on faster. "I'll break all records. We'll be back before you have to saddle up."

All by herself Connie danced and capered like a mad girl. Golden Sovereign wasn't mean, he wasn't a killer, he wasn't a man-hater. He was just misunderstood! "Dear Camellia . . . Please hurry, Pete. Poor Sliver, all this time you just wanted your playmate." It was hard to keep from running into the stallion's stall to tell him that Camellia was coming, but knowing that he didn't know his friend would soon arrive stopped Connie. She snatched the brave green blouse and ducked into a stall to change to Shamrock Stables' colors. A yellow ribbon was tied around her hair, and she danced exuberantly on one foot to polish her boots.

Minutes dragged past and Pete must be nearing the farm, she figured. A half-hour passed—by now Camellia should have been shoved into the back seat and Pete would be speeding back. Another half-hour crawled by, but no sign of Pete. What was keeping him? There'd be lots of Saturday traffic, of course, and congestion near the fairgrounds, but Connie knew Pete could drive like the wind when he wished.

Maybe he'd had an accident! Her heart pinched her, and not because of Camellia or Golden Sovereign. No, it couldn't be an accident; Pete was too careful for that. She looked at her watch to note the passing of another half-hour, but the hands marked only a few minutes gone.

Doc and her father strolled up, having completed their tours of the Fair, and were startled at Connie's wild look of anxiety.

"Pete's gone to get Camellia. Golden Sovereign's lonesome. He should have been back a long time ago. I hope he hasn't had an accident."

They stared at her disjointed conversation, wondering whether the three days' strain might have been too much for her.

"It's time to start getting Golden Sovereign ready, Connemara. Don't worry about Pete—he'll be all right."

"No, don't go in yet. Wait till Pete comes back. He'll be here soon."

They looked at each other in perplexity, and had Mrs. McGuire been there she would have laid a hand across Connie's brow to test it for fever. Gradually Connie made them understand what had happened and why Pete's return was so important. Then their anxiety was added to hers as they watched the entrance in an agony of waiting.

"Listen." Connie cocked an ear toward the highway.

The wail of sirens grew stronger every second

and screeched to a crescendo just around the curve. Connie's heart leaped with joy and relief to see Pete's car swerve through the gate and jounce toward the stables. Outside the sirens muttered complainingly to silence.

"Pete, you're wonderful! Did you get a motor-cycle escort? You're just in time."

"I had a sort of police escort—only they were behind me instead of ahead. Here's your goat. She's kind of shaken up. It was a rough trip, but Golden Sovereign won't mind."

There was but a short time before the race, and heroic measures were necessary. Connie rushed Camellia to the stallion's door and, opening the lower half, she pushed the goat in. Golden Sovereign's half-charge was checked in mid-air, and he dropped his head, a nicker of welcome fluting his nostrils. Camellia bleated once or twice, perhaps in protest at such a sudden change of scene, and her friend nosed her in answer. Silence, the first in three days, descended inside the stable.

Horse and goat were left together until there was just time to saddle up, but even the small dose of Camellia's company had been effective. His door was opened gingerly, and they laughed aloud with relief. The palomino stallion might have been an entirely different horse from the one they had fought with that morning. His eyes looked steadily at them without any rolling whites visible, his ears were set forward in attention rather than lying tight to his head, and his hoofs stayed on the ground instead of flashing in the air.

Connie's hands shook so from reaction that Pete had to take over for her. Doc shortened the stirrups and spoke words of encouragement.

"Don't worry about the other horses, Connemara. That Coleman must know—or thinks he knows—what he's doing, so trail him for the first mile. That's when the weak ones will drop out and the horse that has what it takes will win. Golden Sovereign might be that horse. Good luck!"

From her perch atop the stallion Connie saw faces as a blur, and she felt that she was riding forth alone to adventure. She and the other riders, none of them the owners, met and received their instructions. The race was to start and finish in front of the grandstand and was two laps around the track.

In addition to the red bay owned by Coleman there was another bay, a black, and a chestnut. She tried to figure out which ones might be her biggest threat, but remembering Doc's words, concentrated on her own mount. She missed the feeling of coiled muscles, but hoped it resulted from his change of heart and not from fatigue. Time alone would answer.

Since harness horses do not use a starting gate or wire, it had been agreed that the horses should line up, the starter count one-two-three, and on the fourth beat wave a flag. Golden Sovereign had drawn Number 4 position, one horse outside him and three between him and the rail, which was not good, but since the red horse was fifth and in a worse position, Connie accepted it philosophically.

Every horse was on tiptoe, some wheeled and danced behind the line, but the red horse and Golden Sovereign faced forward. Connie felt the stallion quiver under her, and her own muscles tensed at the count of one. Two!—she caught her breath. Three!—her mind closed out the rest of the world.

"They're off!" the crowd roared as the five horses catapulted forward.

The three on the rail shot into the lead. The black surged ahead and the field strung out behind, Connie and the red horse side by side in the dust. The black's long strides carried him clear out in front, but Connie was not worried, knowing he never could hold such a pace for the distance.

Halfway round the first time she passed the second bay, which was already tiring and dropping back. At the three-quarter pole she noted that the gap between the black and the rest of them was slowly closing, and going past the grandstand into the second lap they were strung out in a line: black, chestnut, bay, and palomino. Golden Sovereign was running easily, and Connie could notice no apparent laboring, though his neck stretched out farther.

The red horse's rider stepped him up suddenly and the black was ahead of them for a minute, only to drop back, done for. Connie was riding with every ounce of skill she had, and she could sense that their moment of decision was near. Red and chestnut were neck and neck at the quarter pole, but the chestnut couldn't take it, and his

head dropped back to the red's withers, his flank—
and then a gap appeared.

Golden Sovereign passed the chestnut easily at
the turn of the track, and Connie knew that the
time had come to challenge the red horse. The
wind whistled past her and the horse's mane flicked
her face like foam, but she was unconscious of
anything but the horse ahead. She called on the
stallion for greater speed, and he answered gal-
lantly.

Stride by stride the gap narrowed between them
and the red horse, but when he heard their thun-
dering hoofs he increased his speed. Golden Sovereign hung on staunchly past the half-mile pole,
and though for a few rods the gap was stubbornly
the same, it didn't widen—almost imperceptibly
golden nose crept up to bay flanks.

At the three-quarter mark a palomino shadow
was cast across the bay and the track straightened
into the home stretch. Both horses were straining
ahead, and it was no longer a matter of speed—
only endurance. Golden Sovereign clung to his position valiantly and hair by hair drew abreast of the
red.

Nose and nose they raced for the finish line,
matching stride for stride with each other. The
red horse's rider was whipping his mount on, and
Connie screamed for more speed. The stallion dug
deep into his past, and from some Arabian ances-
tor, or perhaps from his own deep heart, he responded with a burst of speed.

Connie was vaguely aware of a great roaring in

the distance, as though a flight of airplanes was going over, but she could see no farther than the finish line.

"Come on, Sliver, come on, hi-i-i-ya-ah." Like a thing apart her voice called to the laboring horse, and he found one more notch of speed to give her. That was enough. The red's nose was even with her boot, and his rider's yelling and whipping were useless. In that position they flashed across the finish line.

Their momentum carried them far down the track before Connie could ease the stallion around and return to the judges' stand. Doc was jubilantly hysterical. Pete hugged Golden Sovereign's sweaty shoulder and shook Connie's foot in congratulation. Her father was too busy accepting the winner's purse from the judges to talk to her then, but hundreds of enthusiastic spectators shouted their approval.

"Golden Sovereign, the horse of iron. Golden Iron, he oughta be," someone yelled hilariously.

Connie wrapped her arms around his neck and humbly apologized for all the bad things she had said to him in the past, promising him nothing but praise henceforth. Then, seeing that her father had everything under control, she jerked her head toward the stable and Pete followed at her stirrup.

Many horsemen stopped by to congratulate her and see this horse of golden iron, but Connie was upset by their refusal to believe that Golden Sovereign's disposition had altered overnight.

"I'm greedy, Pete, and want everything. Now

college is assured, I want to re-establish his repu-
tation as a nice, sweet-tempered horse—but nobody'll believe me. They've got to. All of Shamrock Stables depends on it, for unless we prove it
today, Golden Sovereign will have a bad name the
rest of his life."

But the more she talked the more disbelieving
her callers were. When Doc arrived, she called on
him to vouch for the stallion's change of heart, but
he was accused of being partial.

"Doc, I think I had Golden Sovereign entered in
Ladies' Mounts this afternoon. After he gets his
wind back and has a little rest, would it hurt to
ride him in that? Not hard, and I don't care whether
I win anything or not, but I want everyone to see
that he's not the same horse at all that went berserk
yesterday. And Dad can lead Camellia right up to
the gate with him, so we'll have the proof right
with us. Can I?"

The veterinary examined the stallion briefly and
pronounced him fit for another horse-show appearance, particularly as it would be quite a while before Ladies' Mounts was called. Golden Sovereign
was cared for as carefully as a baby, and after he
had been walked enough to cool off to the last
wisp of mane, he was polished and buffed as
though he were pure gold.

"Truly we're just going for the ride in this class,
mannie," she whispered to Golden Sovereign as
they rode forth to further conquests.

Some of the entrants who had not heard that
the stallion was a reformed character cast fright-

ened glances toward Connie and her regal mount, but he was as perfectly behaved as the most docile horse present. They walked and trotted and cantered to perfection, and Connie exulted as the dubious began to watch him with growing admiration.

Riders had to dismount, lead their horses around to prove their gentleness, and mount again from the off side, but Golden Sovereign was always the perfect gentleman. For once Connie was glad that their number was not called for further judging, and she joined the other culls in the center. Here again the stallion was perfectly behaved and stood quietly until they were gated before ribbons were awarded.

"Good going, old fellow. We didn't expect a ribbon this time, for no stallion could really be considered a lady's mount, but we showed them you're a good boy again."

Her hand clapped the stallion approvingly on his shoulder; and had any further proof been necessary, his affectionate whinny to Camellia, who waited outside to greet him, showed that the goat's presence governed his behavior.

CHAPTER TWENTY-SEVEN

ENCUMBRANCE

THE HORSES STARED at Connie's strange garb. Instead of boots, she wore shoes and stockings,
and a skirt had replaced her old riding trousers.
Only her blouse seemed the same.

"It's going to be lonesome away at college without them, Pete. I'm glad now I'm only taking the
short course. Two years oughtn't to be too long.
Say, do you suppose the housemother would mind
if I took just the littlest one with me?"

"Probably not, as long as you didn't want to
keep it in your room; but someone'd be sure to tip
her off that that's what you'd do. And she wouldn't
realize how lucky she was that you were willing to
settle for just one—but then you'd probably come

279

back someday with another waif in tow that you'd resurrected from the glue factory."

"Oh, I don't think so. I think Shamrock Stables is launched well enough now so that it'll go along smoothly. No more of these harrowing incidents for me. I'm a big girl now."

Pete looked his disbelief, but merely said, "Shamrock Stables does seem to be on an even keel at last. Did you say that all the foals have been reserved?"

"Every one but Golden Opportunity, and we're going to keep her, since Lady's so super," Connie nodded vigorously. "A man came the day after the Fair and bought one, to be delivered as soon as they're ready. Another was sold a week later, and just yesterday a man from Texas bought Golden Treasure, but she's not to be shipped for a long time."

They silently savored the thrill of selling a foal as far away as Texas, but Connie soon raced on to another item. "One animal we won't sell, now that we've finally bought her outright and for keeps, is Camellia. Isn't it ridiculous that anything as big and glorious as Golden Sovereign is so dependent on a goat?"

"Whether it is or not, you're lucky you were able to buy her and save yourself a bout with that stallion every time they were separated for a few hours. Did you have any trouble with her owners?"

"Not a bit. I honestly think they were kind of relieved to get her off their hands—and her board bill off their checkbook." Her voice ceased, but her thoughts scurried off to reappear from a different direction.

"I wish now we could buy that farm next door. It'd go into this one just perfectly, but Mr. Brand says the owner wouldn't consider selling. The meanie!"

"What d'ya mean, 'meanie'? Maybe he wants to keep it as much as you want to buy it."

"Maybe, but I'm going to keep working on the agent, and someday the owner may weaken."

"Well, he won't, and there's no use nagging."

"How do you know he won't, smarty? Sa-a-y, come to think about it, how *do* you always seem to know about that farm? Did you—do you mean—?"

Pete nodded guiltily. "I cannot tell a lie—I did, I do, it's mine. You said yourself it was good land, and who am I to dispute a lady's word?"

"It is. That's why I wanted it for Shamrock Stables. What do you need a farm for? You'll be in college for two more years and then go in with your dad."

"I'll need a place to live then, and I kind of like it around here. I'm going to build a house on that hill above the lake. And don't be so impatient— you may still have it in with Shamrock Stables, but it won't be clear title. There'll be one encumbrance on it, if you can stand him."

Connie's eyes swept out across the picture she so loved, sloping hillsides dotted with horses, the barns and stacks, the lake in the background, but this time she didn't stop at the line fence, and her imagination set other buildings against the far hill-side. Two years isn't very long.

"Could be," she murmured, still staring at the present and future.

Pete's mood shifted back to the present. "We'll see it again before the two years are up. If we're going to get you there before they lock you out of the dorm for the first time, we'd better get going. Everything packed?"

Connie turned misty eyes to Pete. "I can't go, Pete, after all. Up until this minute I've thought I could, but I can't leave when the Stables are just taking shape."

"Of course you're going. You know that farming and horse raising these days demand the best methods, and where else are you going to learn 'em?" Pete spoke sharply at first, but seeing Connie's genuine distress his tone grew gentler. "I know it looks hard, but you said yourself it was only for two years. Then we'll both be back, and these horses will still be here, and some new ones too. So buck up, Connie, it's just growing-up pains you're having. Are you all packed?" he reiterated.

"Yes, and strapped down," she quavered. "This way, please, Redcap—or Red Thatch."

Connie took one last look at her old world before turning to go with Pete into a new one of eight-o'clock classes, term papers, campus dances, football games—college.